THE MEAN ONES

THE MEAN ONES

TATIANA SCHLOTE-BONNE

Creature Publishing
Charlottesville, VA

This is a work of fiction. Names, characters, places, and incidents either are the products of the author's imagination or are used fictitiously. Any resemblance to actual persons, living or dead, events, or locales is entirely coincidental.

Copyright © 2025 by Tatiana Schlote-Bonne
All rights reserved.

ISBN 9781951971304
LCCN 2024950329

Cover design by Luísa Dias
Cover artwork by Jocelyn McCall
Spine illustration by Rachel Kelli

CREATUREHORROR.COM
@creaturepublishing

Chapter 1

2023

The dead raven on the doorstep is not a good sign. Its wings are bent at a sharp angle, maggots wriggling between black feathers, eye sockets crawling with ants. I've seen enough death to know an omen when it's right at my feet. But then again, I see, and often hear, fucked up shit that other people can't.

You shouldn't have lived, the bird says in Allie's high-pitched, know-it-all voice, the broken beak moving like a puppet's mouth. *You should've died with us.*

Yes, I should be dead, but here I am: twenty-nine years old and still kicking, and on my way to the only place the voices stay away—the gym.

"Aww," Lucas says behind me. "Poor little guy."

Oh good. He sees the dead raven too. But Lucas doesn't hear

all the voices. I wish it was just one: That would make it manageable. Predictable. Maybe even boring. But the multiple voices catch me off guard. Sometimes it's Blakely, who died first. More often, it's Allie, who died second and slower. Sometimes it's *him*. A man's voice. I don't know who he really is or if he's even real. But I know that his voice is as scary as it is pleasurable, and it comes to me in moments of fear and ecstasy.

Lucas loops his gym bag around his shoulder, his red Mustang chirping as he clicks the keys to unlock it. I nudge the raven with my shoe, off the stairs and onto the grass. I wish we could live someplace with no wildlife, no trees, no grass, nothing that can remind me of the forest. The closest I've gotten was a weekend in Vegas, and even then, I was haunted by a flock of talking pigeons on the Strip, goaded by crying trees in the Bellagio.

The dead raven lies on its back by the driveway, black talons curled. *Should've died with us*, the bird repeats, its head turning so its ant-riddled eye sockets follow me. *Join us.*

"Yeah, whatever," I mutter under my breath, hoping an owl swoops down and eats the chatty carcass for lunch. If I let it be funny that dead animals talk to me in the voices of my murdered friends, then it's not scary. Shit only gets scary when I take it seriously.

I get into the car, turning up the classic rock radio station. Nothing like a good '80s bop to quiet the trauma. Lucas places his gym bag in the back and gets into the driver's seat like everything is normal, because for Lucas, everything *is* normal. He doesn't hear dead animals and trees talking to him, nor does he fall asleep to images of his childhood best friends dying at summer camp.

He doesn't hear the sounds they made—the muffled screams and the *swoosh* of blood spilling, then splattering. I can't clean floors for that reason. The splat of the wet mop on tile, the squelching of the dirty water. The same sounds can come from a little girl's body when her throat is slit.

Lucas backs out of the driveway, turning on the seat warmers to prime our backs for lifting. "You take your creatine?"

"Yep." I remind myself that everything is going to be okay: We're going to the gym. The voices can't reach me with my headphones blasting in my ears and endorphins rushing through my veins.

"Did you take yours?"

"Of course." He squeezes my quad. "Keep growing these thunder thighs, baby."

I laugh, flexing my leg so Lucas can feel the full density of my muscly quad. He loves my legs, and I love that he loves my legs. Once, lying naked in the bathtub, I crushed a watermelon between my thighs—it exploded, splattering from my head to my feet. Lucas cleaned me with his tongue.

I run my hand over Lucas's legs and crotch, heat rising in me. We've been together for three years. Hopefully, he will propose soon. (I'd say yes if he asked me right now at this red light.) We're perfect for each other, or at least, he's perfect for me. The worst thing that ever happened to Lucas: His parents got divorced when he was ten. The eldest son of a stay-at-home essential-oil-shilling mother and a software engineer father, Lucas grew up with little stress, no one ever doubting his abilities or potential for success. He's the prototype of the upper-middle-class white man. He even looks generically handsome, like a man out of a magazine for suits who you'd note as remarkably good looking but whose face would evaporate from your mind the moment you turned the page.

I can see how, from someone else's perspective, Lucas is bland. Heather is always telling me that Lucas is as funny and interesting as unbuttered wheat toast. She's right; I won't even try to deny it because I don't mind that Lucas is boring. In fact, I prefer him this way.

I look over at him, admiring his tousled dirty-blond hair and hazel eyes. When he turns up the AC and says, "It sure is a hot one today," I beam, relishing how simple, how predictable, how fully in the real world Lucas is. I love that he isn't like me at all: scarred, deranged.

Broken.

◎

Once we're at the gym, I head to the locker room. I'm anxious to get lifting, but I have to take a pre-lift piss or else I risk wetting myself during my heavier sets. I drop my leggings and sit on the toilet, wondering if I'll be able to work up to 90 percent on deadlifts today. Maybe even 93 percent, if I'm feeling good. A cold droplet plops onto my forehead. Then another. I look up, hoping it's just a leaking pipe, but I know better.

Allie's on the ceiling, her back against it like she's lying on a bed, her long hair hanging around her face. She looks just like she did when she was alive, except she's translucent, and her arms and chest are marred by stab wounds. Her bottom lip wobbles as she cries, her tears landing on the same exact spot on my forehead, like a ghostly waterboarding. *Plop, plop, plop.* I pull my pants back up, trying not to look at her. *She's not real.* Once I start working out, this will stop.

I wash my hands and rush out of the bathroom in an acceptable I'm-in-a-hurry way, not a running-from-a-ghost way. Allie follows, drifting along the ceiling, her tears still landing on my head with the accuracy of a precision airstrike. I put my headphones in and loop a resistance band around my knees and start lateral sidestepping. Once I'm thirty seconds into a Korn song and my glutes are thoroughly burning, Allie's ghost fades away.

My phone dings in my pocket and I pull it out. It's a new work email.

From Marianne Bennet, Doctor of Physical Therapy:

Can you squeeze in my 3:30 client on Tuesday? He needs soft tissue work and stability exercises for his back pain.

Yes! I reply, and then to show that I'm not burdened by this, that I'm a good physical therapy assistant, that I would prefer to have an increased workload, I add: Anytime! Not a problem at all!

Maybe it was too much, makes me seem too eager. But I've already hit send.

You're the best! Marianne replies a minute later, clearly not overthinking it like me.

I kick off the band and start a set of hip hinges with the empty barbell. What would my life be like if I'd become a real physical therapist instead of settling for being an assistant? I would have more money, but money isn't a terrible issue with Lucas's job as a real physical therapist. I would be busier—*that* was the lamentable part.

The Mean Ones

If I had finished my bachelor's degree and put in the shadowing and internship hours, then I could be a doctor of physical therapy right now. I would be able to stack my schedule with as many patients as possible, barely leaving myself time to have my own thoughts. When I'm busy, the visions and voices are quiet, even sometimes gone entirely.

I load 135 pounds onto the barbell. It wasn't exactly my choice to bail on getting the doctorate: between my dad's colon cancer; and my anxiety, depression, and PTSD-induced hallucinations; I just couldn't keep up with the grades and workload. But then I met Lucas, and he introduced me to powerlifting, and now I have this hobby that releases my endorphins and keeps my mind occupied just enough to keep the bad things at bay.

That's what all the shit I've been through has taught me: You can't escape your past, but you *can* distract yourself from it. You can run away (or in my case: lift).

In the middle of my warm-up sets, the Atreyu song I'm blasting cuts off, replaced by the cloying melody of my ringtone. I continue my deadlifts, ignoring the ringing even though it's killing the vibe and making the weight feel heavier. After I finish my eighth rep, I check my phone. It's Heather. I almost answer the call, but we'll get to speculating about how and when I think Lucas might propose and where we should go thrifting next, and then my muscles will get cold and I'll get distracted from my lifts. I send her a quick message: lifting, will call soon! Then I put my phone on Do Not Disturb.

When I get to my top deadlift sets, Lucas watches me, postponing his own lifts to coach mine. While I chalk my hands, he reminds me of my cues: *pack your lats, pull the slack out, get your air.*

I grip the bar, screw my feet into the floor, suck in a deep breath, and drive through my legs. Over my headphones, I can hear Lucas shouting, "Up, up, up!"

Three hundred pounds comes off the floor heavy but smooth, and when I lock it out, an exhilarating current rushes through me, leaving me feeling lightheaded but powerful, like I could wrestle a lion or pick up a car the way one might lift a moderately heavy box.

Lucas whoops, and once I return the weight to the floor and unlock my belt, he gives me a high five.

"You're killing it, babe." He kisses my forehead.

I smile, blinking the stars from my vision. Behind Lucas, a poster on the wall reads *Colorado Powerlifting Throwdown: July 30th! Register now!*

Maybe I should sign up for that. But then the reality of what it would entail creeps over me—lifting in front of all those people, lifting with women way stronger than I am—and the sensation that I could do anything quickly fades. I look away from the poster, positioning myself so it's not in my line of view anymore. I can't compete. It's too much. Too scary. Too out of my comfort zone. Besides, Lucas will probably compete, and if I did, too, I would be taking the spotlight away from him. I should be there to support him.

Lucas helps me put my plates away, then walks over to the dumbbells, literally strutting, a spring in his step that's almost feminine, but it only seems that way because his legs and glutes are so toned, and they're especially noticeable in his men's workout leggings. Meggings, I call them, and they make his ass look fantastic.

Lucas pumps out chest flys on a bench. It's his chest and shoulder day; that means we'll have sex in front of the mirror later, Lucas flexing and looking at himself as he thrusts into me, his veins and muscle striations protruding like worms trying to escape through his skin. The first time Lucas watched himself in the mirror during sex, I was so repulsed my vagina instantly dried up. I wanted to ask him to stop, to look at me, not himself, but making such a request was unfathomable. Now, the mirror sex has grown on me. It's a quirk I find strangely sexy. Sometimes, I even enjoy looking in the mirror during sex, watching him watch himself.

I sit at the hamstring machine, slowly curling my legs in, then controlling the extension, feeling the burn in the backs of my thighs, envisioning my muscle fibers stretching and growing, like I can aid in their development with my mind. Across the gym, Lucas supersets his chest flys with lateral raises, his broad lats popping through his tank top, then he abruptly sets his weights down and pulls his ringing phone from his pocket. He answers, standing tall, his full attention on the phone.

My stomach flips, my blood pressure rising. Something bad must've happened: A death in the family? A fire that burned our house down and our cats couldn't escape? Why else would he be taking a phone call in the gym?

There's no need to go from 0 to 100, I remind myself in the voice of my ex-therapist. But 0 to 100 is my nature.

Then Lucas laughs. His posture relaxes. He leans against the wall, nodding. I finish my last rep, making sure I give my hamstrings a final good squeeze, then walk over to Lucas to hear what he's saying. What phone call—if not grave news—could interrupt his workout?

"No, bro, we don't have anything going on this weekend. Sadie's off work too," Lucas says, his tone deepening into his bro voice, which he only uses for *Call of Duty* and talking to Eli, his best friend and Heather's husband. Eli says something on the other line, his voice too muffled for me to understand.

"Yeah, man, we'd love to," Lucas responds.

We'd love to *what?*

Go to dinner?

Go to a movie?

Go out to the new bar that just opened on First Ave.?

My mind whirrs with all the possible things Eli could be inviting us to. I don't like unplanned plans—in fact, I loathe them. All activities in my life must be predetermined in my planner, from when I sleep and eat to when I go grocery shopping and watch Netflix. It's how I stay in control. Stay calm. Stay normal. Lucas doesn't understand that I'm in a constant battle to be the version of Sadie Ellis that he knows and loves. Recently, I've been winning this battle. Somedays, I almost believe that I am Normal Sadie Ellis. But now, Lucas could be jeopardizing it all, and for what?

I scoot closer to Lucas, trying to make out what Eli is saying, but it's too loud in the gym. Lucas wraps a sweaty arm around me, our salty skin uncomfortably sticking together.

"Pike Forest?" Lucas says, enthusiasm brimming.

Forest? My heart knocks in my chest, my fingers tingling with anxiety. Surely, Eli isn't asking us to go to a forest. Maybe he's only inviting Lucas. They're having a guy's trip—*that has to be it!*

But with a sickening twist in my stomach, I remember Lucas's words: "*We'd* love to."

I start shaking my head, my whole body saying *No, absolutely not. No no no.*

"Awesome," Lucas says. "I mean, sucks that your parents got sick, but we're down."

We're not down! I scream internally, but how can I tell Lucas this? How can I explain that I can't go to a forest without exposing everything about my past? Besides, when have I ever told Lucas—or anyone—no?

"Hold on—" Lucas says to Eli. "Sadie's right here." He holds the phone to his shoulder. "Babe, Eli's parents rented a cabin, but they got the flu and can't make it, so Heather and Eli want us to come hang with them. Awesome timing, right? It's a three-day weekend."

Yes, it is Memorial Day weekend, but that means Lucas and I are supposed to go out for sushi tomorrow—I already planned it into my macros. We're supposed to sleep in these next few days, spend more time at the gym, and finally recycle all the cans we've been storing in the garage.

I chuckle to conceal my desperation. "I thought we had plans?"

"To do the same stuff we do every weekend? Come on, let's have fun for a change."

"But a forest? There's—"

"There's what? Spiders?" Lucas snickers.

"Yeah. And bears. Remember *Backcountry*—?"

"That guy was a pussy."

"That guy's lips were ripped off his face—"

"I'll protect you." Lucas puts his hand behind my neck, giving it a light squeeze.

I stare into his eyes, willing myself to say no—*just say no!*—but all my mouth forms is a pained little smile that Lucas reads as agreement.

"Let's get home and pack."

I hold his hand on the way to the car, searching for something—anything—that could be a viable excuse, but I have nothing. Besides, it's clear the decision has already been made. Maybe if I did tell the truth, maybe if I told him all the terrible things I've been keeping secret, then he would realize we shouldn't go camping.

But I can't tell him now, not after three years.

I get into the passenger seat, glancing at Lucas. We're perfect the way we are. I can't defile what we have—can't undo this version of myself I've created—by telling him the truth about me.

I can't tell him that the childhood he thinks he knows about me is a lie.

That he doesn't know anything about my past, about my friends who died at camp, about how I let them.

I can't tell him that my real name isn't Sadie.

Chapter 2

2006

"*Camping?*" Mom asked like I'd handed her a pamphlet about a trip to Mars. She flipped through the information pages about seventh-grade summer camp, her reading glasses low on her nose, the way she read all things with small print. "Since when are you interested in camping?"

I was *not* interested in camping. This was back when I went by my birth name, Sabrina. Everyone called me Bina, which I hated. It sounded like a baby's name. Even though I was twelve and the proud owner of A-cup boobs, had hair growing in each armpit, and had produced three clumpy, sporadic periods, I was still "Baby Bina."

"I don't know," I responded to Mom. I couldn't get out of going camping without making Allie mad at me. She was the one who wrote my name on the sign-up sheet last week. "If you don't go camping," Allie said when she told me she'd signed me up, "I'm going to tell everyone about how you're a chicken little pissy pants."

My face reddened, remembering the instance Allie was referring to when we'd been in the ball pit at Chuck E. Cheese and I'd had too much 7 Up. Everyone peed in the ball pit—that's practically what it was for, a place to relieve yourself before racing back up to the top of the indoor jungle gym. If Allie had peed in the ball pit, it would've been cool. But because I did it, it was gross, embarrassing. Allie was always holding things over my head and forcing me to do things I didn't want to, like pushing me forward when Mrs. Peterson asked who would be Meg in our class's performances of *Hercules* (Allie had stage fright and was paranoid Mrs. Peterson was going to pick her), like making me play volleyball instead of soccer (Allie said the outfits were cuter), like signing me up for stupid summer camp (I didn't know her agenda yet, but I suspected she had all kinds of pranks planned).

Still, despite all of Allie's assholery, there was some strange pleasure in having her make decisions for me, and even some stranger pleasure in how my compliancy pleased her. At only twelve years old, I already knew this simple, harsh truth about the world: There were mean girls and there were nice girls, and one couldn't exist without the other.

"Well, I think it's wonderful," Mom said. "You're getting out of your shell! You know, when I was a few years older than you, I had the best time of my life at cheer camp. It was 1982 and I'd just gotten my hair permed..." She took off her reading glasses and drifted into one of her long-winded stories about her teenage glory days, running her fingers through her hair as she talked.

Mom had just gotten her hair done and had thick bleach-blonde highlights like Rachel from *Friends*. In general, Mom looked a lot like Rachel from *Friends*. It's terrible having a hot mom when you're not. Dad was half-Mexican and incredibly hairy, unreasonably so, with tufts of dark curly fur growing all over his back, his shoulders, his feet. I was pale like Mom, yet I'd somehow inherited 100 percent of Dad's hairy gene. Twice a week, I shaved the tiny black mustache hairs growing above my lip.

"Are you listening, Bina?" Mom asked, her blue eyes sharp.

I nodded.

"Good. I'm getting to the best part—Donny Hudson pulled up to our cabin in his red convertible Camaro, blasting Van Halen through the open roof." She walked up the stairs, continuing on about Donny and his leather jacket and how fast his car went, flapping her hand for me to keep up. Pepper, our fluffy black Pomeranian, bounced up the stairs, following closely behind Mom. She paused to look at herself in the mirror, smoothing her hands over her tiny waist clinched in a blue apron. "And that night at camp is when Donny and I had our first kiss," she said dreamily.

We stepped into my room, which was painted a light purple, the walls decorated with *The Lord of the Rings* posters and Pokémon stickers. On the dresser, my pet rats, Nyarro (Elvish for rat) and Radagast, napped on their hammock. Contrary to popular belief, rats are clean rodents. When I first asked for pet rats, Mom refused, ignorantly thinking they would smell up the house and give us the plague. It was Dad who listened to my lectures on rat biology and gave in when I pleaded and begged for them. The rats reminded me of my favorite animal: the opossum, immune to rabies, the adorable eater of ticks. I closed my bedroom door, locking Pepper out so she couldn't try to eat Nyarro and Radagast.

"We stayed under the stars that night by the river," Mom said. "We weren't supposed to, of course. But we were sixteen!" She paused, waiting for my reaction.

"Sounds great." I gave her a forced smile.

"Aww, sweetie." She cupped my cheeks. "I'm so excited for you." Her hands moved to my head where she started flattening my frizzy curls, which immediately sprung back to life once she let go. "You're going to make so many of your own wonderful memories."

I gave her another fake smile.

"Now, let's get you all set with some cute outfits." Mom pulled the suitcase down from the closet, picking out the clothes I would wear at camp, not glancing back to see if I approved.

My fate was clear: There was no getting out of camp. I sat on the bed, my palms growing clammy, my pulse steadily climbing. At camp, there would be bugs.

Spiders.

Wasps.

Ticks.

Ticks meant Lyme disease.

I was what my school counselor called a "hypochondriac," a label I didn't agree with because to me it was just plain smart to be educated and aware of all the bad things that could happen to you. I knew that Marcy Dixon, one of Mom's friends from golf club, got all rashy and had to give up golfing and all the things she enjoyed because she caught Lyme disease from a tick and was in pain all the time.

Mom continued piling shorts and skirts and tank tops into the suitcase—I would need to swap them all out for pants, long sleeves, long socks. I knew I really should just tell Mom that I didn't want to go to camp at all, but I couldn't muster the courage to say no, and even if I could, I wouldn't be able to handle her reaction. She was already so excited about me going, was probably making plans for what to do while I was gone, was probably writing stories in her head about all the things I'd get to do at camp. If I said no, I would be such a disappointment, and then she would just make me go to camp anyway.

The sound of the garage door opening reverberated through the walls. Pepper started barking.

"Dad's home," Mom said. "I'm going to put the lasagna in the oven." She tossed a pair of flip-flops into the suitcase. "Check your bathroom supplies and we'll get whatever else you need from the store."

"Okay," I said, my voice a small squeak.

Mom left my room, her voice echoing up the stairs as she told Dad that I was going to summer camp.

"Really?" Dad said, shocked but pleased. "Well, that's great!"

I crawled under my bed, where I always went when the world felt like too much. With the frame a few inches above my face and the bed skirt draped over the sides, I was invisible to the world, safe and protected in my own dark little cave. I curled into a ball.

Camp can't be too bad, right? It was only two weeks. That was the same time we got off for Christmas break and that went by like nothing.

Just as my heart rate started to slow, the phone beside my bed rang. My heart kicked up again; it had to be Allie. No one else called the house at four in the afternoon.

I reached up from beneath the bed, wrapping my fingers around the springy cord as I brought the phone down into my cave with me. "Hello?"

"Hey, betch," Allie said. "You get the papers signed for camp?"

Chapter 3

2023

The moment we're home from the gym, Lucas passes the kitchen, skips his post-workout banana and protein shake, and goes straight for the closet in the spare bedroom to grab a suitcase. I stand by the dresser, aghast, as he carefully places a variety of joggers into the suitcase.

Why is he so excited about this damn trip? A new fear stirs inside me: What if the very repetitiveness of our daily lives that I love so much—Lucas hates? What if I don't know him at all?

No. I remind myself that *he* is the one who doesn't really know *me*.

Lucas holds up a pair of running shoes and cross-training shoes, trying to choose between them, then shrugs and puts both in the suitcase. "Eli said we should head there right now." His voice brims with excitement. "Then we can get up first thing in the morning and have the whole day."

"*What?*" We have to leave *right now*? It's 6 p.m. "We can't just go in the morning? What about the cats?"

I gesture at Kilo and Barbell, who are curled up on the bed.

"I'll ask Suzanne to stop by and check on them."

The thought of our retired neighbor cat sitting makes me feel a little better, but I still do not want to go on this spontaneous trip.

"Can you pack the protein powder?" Lucas asks, placing several pairs of socks into the suitcase. "We should take the pancake mix too. Eli said there's a full kitchen."

"Why are you so excited about going?" I blurt, then smile to not seem defensive. Lucas's limit is about three questions before he starts getting irritable and feels "interrogated," and I'm nearing my question allowance. It's time to backtrack a little. I say my next words extra softly: "I just didn't know you were so into camping."

"I used to go as a kid." Lucas adds a few pairs of his underwear to the suitcase. "You should bring a good pair of shoes. Eli and I are planning to go hiking and fishing."

This really is just a guy's trip for Lucas. So why do I have to go at all? I suppose that since Heather is going, I'm expected to go, too, or else Heather will be the third wheel. But Heather's tough; she could handle that. I search for a way to suggest that I stay behind, that I'll just get in the way. "You know I'm no good at hik—"

Before I can finish my sentence, Lucas is gripping my hips, speaking into my ear, his trimmed beard brushing my cheek.

"And I've never seen you out in the wild." He kisses my neck. "I want to see you catch a fish. Watch this ass climb a tree." He squeezes my butt.

If I really were Normal Sadie Ellis, this would be exciting. A happy romantic getaway. And more than anything, I want to be that person. I want to not just *pretend* to be Normal Sadie Ellis, but actually *be* her and forget that Sabrina-I-Watched-My-Friends-Die-Evans ever existed at all.

I close my eyes, leaning into Lucas's embrace, envisioning that I really am Normal Sadie: the girl who lived a quiet, uncomplicated childhood in Cedar Rapids, Iowa, whose biggest problem was her dad getting cancer when she was in college, whose dream in life has always been to get married and have a nice, modest house; several pet rats; and one human baby.

Normal Sadie would love an outdoors weekend getaway with Lucas, and to really *be* her, isn't it time I start making Normal Sadie choices? It's not like it's even the same forest I went to in middle school. We're going to Pike Forest, Colorado—it's a world away from Graywood Forest, Alabama. Plus, I'm an adult now. A buff adult with watermelon-crushing thighs. And I have Lucas by my side. Now that I'm really thinking about it, maybe my initial refusal to go was an overreaction.

Lucas kisses me, nibbling my bottom lip. I return his kiss, lacing my fingers behind his neck. He grips my lower back, pulling me into him, pressing me against his firm chest. It's like hugging marble. Damp, salty marble. "Let's shower?" I ask.

Lucas follows me to the bathroom, pulling his shirt off, exposing his myriad of abdominal muscles. I turn on the water as hot as it will go, then we step inside. Lucas lathers a loofah, gently scrubbing it over my back, across my breasts and arms, making my skin slippery. Steam fills the room, the shower doors fogging over. I shampoo my hair while Lucas rubs his chest with his new soap. A smoky scent fills my nostrils. The hairs on my neck raise. The smoky scent thickens, evolving into the harsh smell of burnt hair and blood, acrid and metallic. I swallow back a gag.

It's the same horrible smell I was trapped breathing in the night Allie and Blakely died.

"What's wrong?" Lucas asks, washing his armpits. "You don't like my new soap?"

I read the label. *Men's Soap: Gunpowder with Activated Charcoal.*

It's the smell of the soap triggering my memories. I laugh. Just dumb man soap from Bath & Body Works. "It's nice," I say. "Potent."

I keep trying to ignore the scent, but the soap is making my throat burn, my eyes water, and I know the smell I'm smelling isn't really Lucas's soap. No. This is what my stupid brain does: It dramatizes every little thing and links every detail it can back to that night at camp. *Stop it*, I plead.

I close my eyes, letting the hot water blast me in the face. The smell eases. I take a step back, blinking the water out of my eyes, but something worse than the smoky scent is happening.

The grout in the tile darkens, turning from off-white to a blackish brown. My stomach sinks. *Not now. Not in front of Lucas.*

But it's too late. I'm already going to the Other Place.

It always starts with a familiar smell, sound, or bad feeling, and then my surroundings peel away, and I'm in the same room except it's different: darker and hazier, and things that were on the left are on the right, and sometimes there's blood and body parts hanging from the ceiling and walls.

I sound insane, I know. I probably am.

Aside from some of my previous therapists, I've never told anyone about the Other Place, especially not Lucas. How many times, when chatting with his friends about one of their girlfriends, have I heard him say "don't stick your dick in crazy"? Enough to be sure that he can never know about my Other Place.

I lean against Lucas, who's kissing my neck like nothing weird is happening at all. The shower steam has turned red, a bloody mist in the air. The soap that was on the right is now on the left. The floor beneath my feet, which moments ago was hard and textured to prevent slipping, has turned soft, like freshly turned soil. I look down and see that I'm right: I'm standing on dirt, thin dead branches growing around my feet, brown vines curling upward between my toes.

I turn to face Lucas. He squeezes his conditioner bottle—clumpy blood oozes out. The bloody mess darkens his hair, a slimy string of flesh stuck to the back of his hand. He smiles at me, streams of red running down his face, staining his teeth. *It's not real. Soon it will all be over.*

This transition to the Other Place used to terrify me, but that's when I was a kid, weak and afraid of everything. Now that I've been going to the Other Place for seventeen years, I'm not afraid of it anymore. It might look scary, but nothing bad has ever happened here. Sometimes, I even feel strangely safer here than in the real world. Protected. Sometimes, when I'm alone, I even look forward to going here.

It's where *he* is.

Lucas's hand slides between my legs. I gasp. His fingers are slippery, touching me gently, flicking quickly.

Come to me, Sabrina, the voice in my head says. His tone is husky, almost a growl. The disembodied voice in my head never told me his name is Damon; I am the one who named him. The name feels right. It's sexy. Mysterious.

Come to me, Damon repeats. His voice sends pleasurable goose bumps across my skin, and I shudder. Lucas takes this as a sign that he's doing the right thing (he is).

I'm sure that Damon's voice, the way I journey to this other world, the talking dead animals—these are all signs of my insanity. I used to be certain that I had a tumor pressing on some crucial part of my brain, but all my scans have come back clean. My blood cell count is normal. The therapists I've been through have all assured me that the "Other Place" is just PTSD, my brain projecting images to cope with the trauma. One therapist suggested that Damon is part of my subconscious, my "inner voice" who says my most honest thoughts that I can't say out loud. Some days, that makes sense.

You're so beautiful, Damon says.

Lucas spins me around so my back is pressed against his chest, his left hand cupping my breast, the right still rubbing me below. I grip his shoulder, leaning into his touch.

But I never really told that therapist the whole truth, how Damon first spoke to me the night I watched Allie and Blakely die, how he says things that I would never think to myself.

You deserve everything, Damon says. *You deserve the world.*

How when Damon's voice isn't in my head, I miss him.

He is my dirty, demented little secret.

Chapter 4

2006

On the bus to Camp Graywood, I sat by myself while Blakely and Allie sat together in the seat in front of me. It wasn't really their fault that I had to sit alone—they said the three of us couldn't all fit in the same row, which I didn't think was meant to be a dig at my weight. (Still, it felt like one.) And they were right: Only the stick-figure girls and boys could fit together.

I wanted to read a book; my backpack was full of them, but I couldn't read on the bus without getting nauseous. And the only thing that could be worse than being trapped on this long bus ride to camp was puking on the long bus ride to camp. So instead, I clicked through songs on my iPod, searching for something good to help pass the time, a soundtrack that would bring my daydreams to life.

The Mean Ones

I glanced over my shoulder toward the back of the bus where Jesse Pierce sat. He rummaged around in his backpack, his light brown hair hanging over his eyes—his green, perfect eyes. My face warmed at the sight of him. Jesse was so cute he could've been a Disney star, the third younger brother of Cole and Dylan Sprouse. Jesse's head started to move up. I snapped forward, looking down.

In front of me, Allie and Blakely giggled. I clicked on Avril Lavigne's "My Happy Ending" and turned up the volume, trying to drown out their laughter. But it didn't erase the fact that Allie and Blakely were still crouched together, their heads low, whispering and periodically cackling. My stomach clenched.

My mind wandered to a conversation I heard between Mom and one of her friends when I'd been finishing getting ready to go on the camping trip: "I hope Bina can manage to have fun," Mom had said. "But it's hard because she's the third wheel. That's why girls should never be friends in threes. Two always pick on the third. I keep telling Bina to lose the fat, then Allie and Blakely will see her as an equal. She's prettier in the face than them. Poor Allie has a pig nose. No, it's not baby fat. Bina's already had her first period. She has two options: lose the fat or be a loser."

I wrapped my arms around myself, pinching my sides. The worst part of it? I didn't really think I was fat. I studied weight charts and pictures of fat bodies on the internet and while, yes, I was at the upper limit of my weight chart, I was only one pants size larger than Blakely. My shoulders were broader, my rib cage wider. I was simply bigger than Allie and Blakely. Not *fatter*. But Allie and Mom were the ones with opinions that mattered, and so if they said I was fat, then I was.

The bus turned and slowed around a bend, the trees growing into a dense wall of green. I shuddered thinking of all the bugs and infectious horrors that must live within. Thankfully, I'd brought enough insect repellant for a year, in addition to my long sleeves and pants, and that fact made me feel superior to the cool kids. I might've been uglier and fatter, but I was smarter; I was in control of my health; I was fighting a war against bugs.

When the bus went over a bump that made the loud, obnoxious kids shout and scream, I stole another glance back at Jesse. He was too beautiful to ever like a frizzy-haired fat girl like me. Still, I could admire him from afar.

But then I noticed something that made my heart triple backflip: Jesse was sitting hunched forward, elbows on his knees, reading a *book*.

Cute boys did not read.

Cute boys especially did not read the same books I read.

Jesse's book was propped against the backrest of the seat in front of him, but I only needed to see the corner of the red cover to know that it was *Eldest*, the second book in *The Inheritance Cycle*. Jesse's eyebrows furrowed in concentration. He smirked at something—I suspected I even knew what scene it was, considering he was about a third into the novel. My limbs and face tingled, and I felt a primal pull in my chest toward Jesse, like a rope had grown from my heart to his and with each beat it shortened.

Here was the most beautiful boy alive reading a book that I had read, twice. We had something to talk about, to bond over, if I could find the courage.

I will *talk to him*, I promised myself. *I will I will I will I will.*

Blakely had a boyfriend, a rich kid who was in Italy this summer. Allie didn't have a boyfriend currently; she was the proud ex-girlfriend of three boys at our school, all who she had kissed, with tongue! When would it be my turn? I was tired of always waiting for the good things to happen to me, only for them to happen to Blakely or Allie instead.

Then the scary thought occurred: What if instead of waiting for Jesse to notice me, I made it happen?

The thought sent my heart racing, made my hands sweaty.

If I had to be at this stupid summer camp because Allie and my mom made me, then I had to make the most of it, didn't I? Jesse shifted his weight, and when he glanced up, I didn't turn away this time. For half a second, our eyes met. By the time I waved, he was already back in his book. But it was okay, because once we got off this bus and the opportunity presented itself, I was going to talk to Jesse Pierce.

He was going to be my boyfriend.

Chapter 5

2023

I leave the key under the mat for our neighbor to stop by and check on our cats, then Lucas and I get on the road for the two-and-a-half-hour drive. While we merge onto the freeway, I google "Pike Forest, Colorado," searching for evidence that it's a dangerous place where people go missing or get stabbed to death or die in other terrible, inconclusive ways. The results display ads and reviews for Pike Forest's hiking, fishing, mountain biking, and caving. Obviously, we're not going caving. I've seen *The Descent*.

I google "Pike Forest Murders," thinking more specifics might help. The first few articles are about shootings in an Ohio area called Pike County. I scroll down. More towns with the word *Pike* in the name, some horror movie references. I open an article titled "Top Ten Most Deadly Forests."

1. Black Forest, Germany. *Campers Hear the Screams of the Dead at Night*
2. Belanglo State Forest, Australia. *Seven Hikers Butchered by a Gruesome Killer*
3. Aokigahara Forest, Japan. *The Yūrei Live Here: Join Them if You Dare*
4. Graywood Forest, Alabama. *What Happened to Allie Murray and Blakely Edgerton?*

My heart rate spikes; I swipe out of the web page. Of course opening a listicle about deadly forests would turn up the Graywood case. That was stupid of me.

I drop my phone back into my purse, a headache forming behind my brow, my stomach churning. If only I'd outgrown my reading-induced car sickness. I close my eyes, resting my head against the window's cool glass. I'll just have to trust that Pike Forest is going to be safe and normal, and why wouldn't it be?

For the first hour of the drive, Lucas listens to one of his favorite bodybuilding podcasts. This episode is about mental toughness. Two men and a woman discuss how during Arnold Schwarzenegger's glory era, he trained for five hours a day, regularly took ice baths, and woke throughout the night to drink protein shakes, caring for his muscles the way a mother would a newborn.

"To be a real champion," the podcast host says, "it takes sacrifice. You have to train your mind to be stronger than your emotions."

Lucas nods so emphatically it's like he's a devoted Christian listening to a sermon. I hold back a snort. Lucas has the mental toughness of a toddler. Once, I watched him hurl, and consequently break, his phone when he failed a deadlift, then get mad all over again when he found his shattered phone. Rather than witness this blatant cause and effect, Lucas bellowed "And now my phone's broken too!" like it was an act of God that had broken his phone and not his very own hand.

But who am I to judge his lack of maturity? I nearly had an emotional collapse over the prospect of having to go camping. I can hardly approach a tree without risking a panic attack. My mental toughness is just as bad as, if not worse than, his.

"We hired a new PT at the clinic," Lucas says when the podcast ends. "His résumé isn't all that impressive, but the rest of the staff like him. He's Latino, speaks Spanish. Shelly thinks he'll expand our clientele base, and I agree, it's great to have someone who's bilingual on the team, but I'm not too sure about his PT skills. He can't even do a kettlebell swing correctly. And he went to *state* school." Lucas says the word *state* like it's so beneath him.

My eyes narrow, insecurity twisting through me. I went to community college. Does Lucas look down at me for that? Probably. But maybe I'd feel the same if I'd gone to Dartmouth for undergrad and Northwestern for a doctorate. I don't know what to add to this conversation—Lucas is the Ivy League doctor, the business owner. I'm just a PT assistant with an associate's degree. So, I smile and parrot his words back to him, agreeing that, yes, it sounds bad to hire a physical therapist who can't do a kettlebell swing.

That's how Lucas and I met: physical therapy. Three years ago, right after I finished my degree and landed my first job, Lucas visited my clinic to give a demonstration on dry needling. I was twenty-six, scrawny, and chronically worried that I didn't know anything; Lucas was twenty-nine, and the owner of a brand new five-star clinic. He was so handsome: six foot three, his teeth dazzlingly white, his light blue long-sleeved shirt snug around his muscular shoulders and arms. He looked like a fairy tale prince who'd come to life from an animated film and put on an outfit from H&M.

All the other women, the gay receptionist, and I gathered around Lucas, ogling, our collective pining raising the temperature in the room. When Lucas asked for a volunteer, everyone's hand shot up.

He picked me.

My knee had been aching for a while—all those box jumps and burpees at CrossFit—and the treatment would be a bonus on top of getting close to this beautiful man. I sat on the table and pointed to the spot where my knee hurt.

"And now I'll palpate the area," Lucas said to the group. "Test the range of motion." He had me extend my knee, his fingers prodding the tendon beneath my skin. Lucas and I locked eyes: his were hazel, the light brown irises flecked with dashes of green. His eyebrows were flawless, not a hair out of place—I was sure he had to pluck and shape them. (I've since learned that, yes, Lucas does pluck his eyebrows.) I'd never met a man who practiced such self-care.

He held a needle thinner than one used for sewing and stuck it into my quad, a few inches above my knee. I had expected it to sting like a flu shot, but it was painless, barely even noticeable.

"Now, I'll stimulate the myofascial trigger point," Lucas announced. "This increases blood flow and breaks up the tight tissue." He swiveled the needle; my muscle twitched and contracted out of my control. It was a strange feeling: Lucas directing my muscle fibers with this tiny piece of metal, like I was a marionette and he the puppeteer.

"For the quadriceps, we leave the needle in for one minute while the muscle relaxes," Lucas told the room, watching the seconds count down on a stopwatch. He plucked the needle from my knee and a tiny droplet of blood formed. "How does it feel?"

I extended my leg. My knee did feel better, looser but tender. "Good. Thank you."

He smiled and my heart leapt. Then he wiped the bloody spot on my knee and put a small Band-Aid on it, which wasn't necessary since the bleeding had already stopped, but he placed the Band-Aid on so tenderly, smoothing the edges, that I felt precious, like a cherished, delicate doll.

After Lucas finished answering questions and packed up his equipment, he approached me at the desk and asked for my number.

I couldn't believe it. My insides churned with insecurity, my mind reverting to the tween days of incessant bullying. Had someone bribed Lucas to do this? Did Gary the receptionist think it would be funny to get the hot doctor to ask out the lowly assistant? I'd been asked out on dates before, of course, had had boyfriends and sex, lots of it. But it was with men who were frequently unemployed, had facial asymmetries, and were occasionally described by others as "slow." Never someone like Lucas.

"I was thinking we could get dinner sometime," Lucas continued. "I know a nice steak joint downtown. Owner's a buddy of mine from college…" He kept talking, and I realized he wasn't joking. Of course he wasn't, because to Lucas, I was a professional—sane—and even attractive adult. My hair was straightened, and I'd recently gotten my dye job retouched: dark brunette with subtle red highlights. My bangs were freshly trimmed, and I was wearing my usual burgundy lipstick. One of my clients had told me earlier in the day that I looked like a young Selma Blair.

"Yes." I grinned, feeling ridiculous for thinking Lucas could've been pulling some mean, childish prank. "I'd love to." I told him my number, which he typed into his phone.

"Sweet." He winked on his way out the door.

I blushed from my cheeks to my nipples.

After work, I practically skipped to my car, imagining calling one of my girlfriends and gushing: "I met the hottest man at the clinic today. He dry needled me. Then he asked for my number." There would be long squealing and screaming. But I had no girlfriends. No friends at all really, not since camp. Acquaintances, sure. But there was no one in my life who I could call and gush to. Before Lucas, I was alone. I'm only close with Heather now because Lucas introduced us.

Whenever his man tantrums seem like they might be too much, I remind myself of this fact: Without Lucas, I have no one.

Chapter 6

2006

The bus lurched to a stop, the sudden jolt waking me from a nap I hadn't realized I'd slipped into. I sat up straight, rubbing my eyes, and looked out the window at the place where I'd be stuck for the next two weeks. A large wooden sign posted on the grass read CAMP GRAYWOOD in yellow letters. Behind the sign, a gravel path curved through the trees, leading to a hill with a row of small wooden cabins. All around me, the bus buzzed with excited chatter amongst the other kids.

"It's so pretty," a girl squealed.

"Which cabin do you think we'll be in?"

"Where are the boys staying?"

"Are there bears here? Mountain lions?"

"Shut up! I'm scared."

"What if wolves come at night?"

"Calm down," Leilani Thatcher's mother said, one of three parents who'd volunteered to chaperone. Leilani's mother announced that the wildlife was safe. "There are no big bad wolves coming to get you at night." She held her hands up like claws and made a gesture that was supposed to be funny or scary, but it just made everyone on the bus cringe. Leilani's freckles disappeared, her neck turning as red as her cheeks.

The bus doors opened, and we all hurried off, eager to stretch our legs and get outside. On the sidewalk, I stood beside Allie and Blakely as the bus driver opened the storage compartment and passed out our luggage. Allie wandered off to talk to another girl from our class.

"I'm glad you came," Blakely said. Her auburn hair, which had been down before we'd gotten on the bus, was now pulled back in a French braid thanks to Allie. She never braided my hair. But maybe that was because my hair was too thick, too frizzy, too much to deal with, not silky and easy like Blakely's hair, and so it wasn't really Allie's fault, but my own for not having more braidable hair.

"Me too," I lied. "I'm glad my mom let me come."

Blakely was the one who was nice to me more than half the time, and part of me did want to spend time with her. Maybe Allie could trip and fall and break her leg and get sent home, then it could just be me and Blakely.

"I feel, like, bad for Leilani," Blakely said, shuddering. "Having your mom here at camp? Could you imagine?"

Leilani's mom licked her thumb and wiped something off her

daughter's cheek.

"God, no," I said. "You think she's going to spoon-feed her at dinner too?"

Blakely snickered. "She'll probably whip out a boob and breastfeed her."

I laughed and laughed and it felt good to talk shit about another girl. Empowering. But that good feeling fizzled away. Was this how Allie and Blakely talked about me? But just for a moment, it was nice to dip into the cool-girl world that Allie and Blakely were so firmly a part of, to be on the right side of the shit talking.

Leilani's mom led all us kids up the gravel path, where six camp counselors stood holding signs. There were three male counselors and three women. A young, pretty Black woman with long, silky, dark hair held a sign that read *Girls Cabins 1-3*. A lean and tan wrinkly older woman with springy gray curls held a sign that read *Girls Cabins 4-6*. A large middle-aged white woman in khaki shorts pulled tight over her big dimply legs held a sign that read *Girls Cabins 7-10*.

"Look at her thighs," Allie whispered.

"Like cottage cheese," Blakely replied.

I forced a small laugh, pulling at the edges of my shorts.

"Listen for your name and cabin number, then line up accordingly," the Black woman said. Her name tag read Tonya. Kids were still talking, not paying attention. Tonya tucked the sign under her arm and clapped her hands. "If y'all want to have fun, you better quiet down and line up!" Tonya's tone dropped from playful to stern. "You want ice cream? You want to swim in the lake? Then behave."

The crowd hushed.

I already knew that Allie, Blakely, and I were rooming together: We'd requested so in the paperwork, but I had no idea what cabin we'd be staying in. I hoped Tonya would be our camp leader. She had a cool-girl edginess that I could only have in my daydreams.

But Cottage Cheese Legs called our names. Allie groaned and dramatically threw her head back.

Our counselor's real name was Ruth, and we followed her up the hill. She smelled like bananas and had white smears of sunscreen on her shoulders.

"Bathrooms and showers are in that building," Ruth said, her voice tired and humorless with a slight Southern twang. She pointed to a gray building that looked like a truck rest stop. "It's smack dab in the middle of cabins five and six, so y'all at the end have a bit of a hike to get there."

We followed Ruth up the hill to cabins seven through ten. I hoped we would be in cabin seven so we'd be closer to the bathrooms, but no, we were in cabin ten. The farthest from the others.

"All righty." Ruth stopped in front of our cabin, writing on a clipboard. The sun beat down on my face. My shirt was stuck to my back with sweat. I just wanted to get inside and cool off.

"You gals are lucky to get cabin ten," Ruth said as she opened the door.

Hot, humid air gushed out. I looked around for an AC unit but there was none. I groaned. Jesse better fall in love with me or this really would be the worst two weeks of my life.

"Way out here," Ruth continued, "you're closest to nature. Deer will come right up to your window."

"Great," Allie deadpanned. "Because I'm Snow White and that's what I've always wanted."

Blakely laughed. I pretended to not have heard Allie. I felt bad for Ruth, though she looked unaffected. She probably dealt with bratty little girls all the time.

"Twenty minutes to get settled," Ruth snapped. "Then we meet at the bottom of the hill. Bring your swimsuits. Ya hear, princess?" Ruth turned and walked away before Allie could deliver a comeback.

Inside the cabin, we opened the windows, and a slight breeze cooled the room by half a degree. Allie immediately claimed the bed closest to the window, staking her territory by dumping the contents of her pink duffle bag onto it.

There was no sink, no bathroom, so we really would have to hike down the hill to brush our teeth or do anything that required water. I flopped onto the cot farthest from Allie and Blakely, staring up at the ceiling. Even prisoners had a better setup.

The mattress beneath me felt stiff with firm padding, like the kind of mat we used in gym class when we practiced tumbles and cartwheels. I stuck my finger under the sheet and was pretty sure it was made of the same material.

"The boys' cabins aren't too far away," Allie said, sitting cross-legged on her bed, head turned to look out the window. "I'm totally going to sneak out and see Seth." She started putting on sparkling pink lip gloss.

I kept fiddling with the mattress. I didn't want to break any rules, but what if I could sneak out and see Jesse? A daydream of a romantic walk with him unfolded in my mind. I saw us together at night, holding hands, the air misty, dew dripping off the leaves as we explored the woods together like a scene out of *Eragon*. My face flushed and my cheeks tightened into a smile.

"I wish Logan was here." Blakely sighed. "I can't believe his parents dragged him to Venice." She scowled and rolled her eyes.

"What about you?" Allie shot a hair tie at me. "Which boy do you like? And what are you smiling about?"

My face dropped. "Nothing. And I dunno." If I confessed my crush on Jesse, it would be just like Allie to go and tell him to embarrass me. But then again—maybe it wouldn't be the worst thing for Allie to break the ice for me like that. Even though I wanted to talk to Jesse, promised myself I would, I wasn't sure I would really go through with it. And that was the sick truth about my friendship with Allie: As long as I had her, I didn't really have to do the hard things. She could do them for me.

"Don't tell us you're a dyke," Blakely said.

"Eww!" Allie shrieked.

I jolted, surprised that this comment came from Blakely and not Allie. Blakely only got mean like this when she was trying to impress Allie, but part of me understood. Allie's approval was rare, and she loved a good burn.

"No," I said. "I like boys. A boy. You probably don't even know who he is."

Allie moved across the room to sit beside me. "What's his name? And why don't we do something nice with your hair?" Allie ran a hand over my frizzy locks. "It's so thick and pretty."

I stifled a gasp, my cheeks glowing. Allie thought my hair was pretty?

Allie sat behind me, running her fingers through my tangles. I could feel her hands working my hair into a braid, the weaving back and forth undoing my tension, like her hands were unlocking me. "I like Jesse Pierce," I blurted without even thinking.

"Who is that?" Allie asked.

"He's a seventh grader and has hair like Dylan Sprouse," I said. "He's in Mr. Barnes's science class."

"Ohhh." Blakely nodded. "Yeah, he's cute."

"Wait," Allie said, holding my hair. "Does he hang out with David Miller?"

"I think so," I said.

"Yeah, he is cute." Allie continued my braid. "He's here at camp, right?"

I nodded.

Allie tied off the end of my hair, then scooted forward so she was sitting next to me. She took the lip gloss out from her pocket. "Put this on."

I obeyed and smeared the gloss, still warm from Allie's pocket, across my lips.

"Damn, Bina," Blakely said. "You look hot."

I blushed. Allie gave me an approving nod and fixed one of my flyaway hairs, and all the hatred I'd ever felt for her immediately dissolved. Allie had this special ability to be lovable mere minutes after she'd been detestable, and even though I regularly told myself that as soon as I got to high school and had the freedom to find a whole new group of friends, I would never speak to Allie again, I knew that part of me wanted, needed—might have even been addicted to—Allie and her bullying. She was the prettiest girl at our school, all the boys wanted to date her, and we were all jealous of her silky, naturally platinum-blonde hair. I was lucky to be her friend.

Allie pulled her Nikon camera out from her bag, gesturing for Blakely to sit at my other side. Allie held the camera up, the lens facing toward us. I grinned. The lens clicked and the flash blinded us, but we kept smiling. Allie brought the camera down, showing us the picture on the little screen.

"Aww," Blakely said.

"Can you email this once we're home?" In the picture, my lips were the same glittery pink as Allie's, my hair braided just like Blakely's. Allie made duck lips while Blakely and I smiled.

If a stranger looked at the picture, they would think I was one of the cool girls, one of the hot girls—they might even think I was the Hot Girl, our leader, instead of Allie, and because of that, this picture would briefly be my favorite, but those same things I loved about the picture would soon come back to haunt me when it was plastered all over the news. The lip gloss would be picked apart by the media, the angle of my smile scrutinized, the glint in my eye misread as something evil.

The picture would become the default image beneath all sorts of headlines:

Are Your Children Worshipping the Devil?

Satanic Cult: Girl (center) Youngest Recruit? Are Our Children Safe?

Girl (center) Watches Friends (left, right) Be Brutalized—Did

She Help the Culprits?

But that first morning we arrived at camp, I adored this picture.

Chapter 7

2023

An hour and a half into the drive to Pike Forest, the city is behind us, the expansive mountains and woods ahead. I hold Lucas's hand as we drive down a two-lane stretch of highway, the only other vehicle a logging truck following slowly behind. The trees grow denser, the sun disappearing behind the mountains.

Lucas talks about the plans for his training in the bodybuilding offseason, something about new equipment for the clinic. I nod along, not really hearing him. The trees look just like the trees we'd passed on the way to camp seventeen years ago: pine trees, maybe? Do the same trees grow in Colorado and Alabama?

Even the way the road is winding feels oddly familiar. The unsettling sensation of déjà vu creeps over me. I've never been out in this direction before, but my body remembers something, knows that it's going to a place it should not.

Lucas slows to turn around a bend. Illuminated by the headlights, the tree trunks look like they're morphing, the dark places in the bark growing and stretching, turning into gaping mouths twisting in pain. If I were Normal Sadie, I would think this is just a trick of the mind—pareidolia, my ex-therapist called it, a perfectly normal occurrence in which people see faces in everyday objects—except, I can *hear* the trees too.

Shrill, mournful wails come from those gaping mouths. The sounds follow me, growing louder as Lucas drives.

Why didn't you save us? a tree sobs. I jolt—it's Blakely's voice, the tone low and throaty.

Another tree up ahead answers: *Because she's a chicken little pissy pants.* It's Allie's voice, sassy as ever.

Allie's laughter comes from the mouth of another tree, and then they're all laughing and crying, a cacophony of echoing voices in my head. I pull my hand from Lucas's, resisting the temptation to cover my ears. If I cover them, then Lucas will realize something's wrong, and I can't let him know that I hear voices in the trees. Normal Sadie does not hear voices from trees.

I stiffen, staring down, focusing on a crumpled receipt at my feet. *That receipt is real. The trees with their mouths and their cries and laughter are not.*

Beside me, Lucas is still talking, but his words are drowned out by the screaming and laughter from the trees. All at once, the voices go quiet. The abrupt silence gives me pause. Why did it stop? Lucas continues his conversation with himself, but his words are distorted, unprocessed by my brain.

I glance up to see if the trees have returned to normal. The headlights shine on a tall thing standing in the road. A dead deer, reared up on its hind legs like a human, except its right leg is mangled, and so it leans its weight to one side. The deer's head hangs to the left, bloody bones piercing through the flesh of its neck. Its abdomen is split open, glistening pink intestines draping around its lower half.

Join us, the deer says in a deep male voice. Damon. I feel a prickle of joy at the sound of his voice, but this is not the time or place.

Lucas is driving straight for the dead deer. When we're yards away from it, I can make out the maggots wriggling in its open flesh, the flies buzzing where its eyes should be. Part of me is tempted to grab the wheel and steer us clear of the thing, but I'm used to this kind of shit by now.

We're not going to crash into the deer because the deer isn't real. Still, I close my eyes, bracing for impact.

Join us, the deer says.

The trees start up again: *Join us, join us, join us.*

I can't help it anymore—I cover my ears. *Toes, ankles, knees*, I recite, flexing each small muscle. This is a grounding technique my ex-therapist taught me, a way to bring myself back down to earth when I'm losing control. It's not very effective, but for a moment, the voices do quiet.

"Have you heard a fucking word I've said?" Lucas snaps. "Are you covering your ears? Do I annoy you that much?"

"Huh?" My head shoots up. The road is clear. "Sorry. I was just…" I glance in the rearview mirror: There's no deer standing in the road anymore. Instead, there's just the lump of a run-over deer lying beside the highway, the roadkill my demented brain reanimated. Still, my body trembles. It's been a long time, but I've seen that deer before. I've tried to forget the broken neck, the way it stood on one leg.

"I know you didn't want to go on this trip, but I thought you'd come around." Lucas shakes his head. "If you're going to be in a shitty fucking mood the whole weekend, then I really should've left you home."

His words sting but I deserve them: I'm ruining the trip before it's even begun. I twist the edge of my shirt, trying not to look out the window, afraid of what I will see. Maybe I shouldn't have quit the pills my doctor gave me, but they didn't help much—the dead animal visions were less frequent (every other day instead of every day), my trip to the Other Place duller. (I still went there, but the world didn't change as much; Damon's voice was weaker.) Overall, the same things still happened, so what was the point in taking pills if they barely changed my imaginary hell and made aspects of my real world—brain fog, appetite, orgasms—worse.

"I'm just tired," I say, my voice flat. I know I should speak sweeter to Lucas, but I can't summon the energy.

"Uh-huh." Lucas's knuckles whiten around the steering wheel. His foot presses down on the gas pedal.

I reach out to touch his arm. He yanks it away.

The speedometer climbs from 75 mph to 85 mph. What is he possibly this mad about? Yes, I'm a Debbie Downer. Yes, from his perspective, I'm moping about the trip, and sure, part of me is—still, how can he get this inexplicably angry?

Three years and I still haven't figured it out, but I've known he can be this way since our fifth date. We went to a nice Italian restaurant and our waitress, clearly flustered on a busy, understaffed night, brought Lucas the wrong drink. He sent it back—the waitress apologized, but then she forgot to bring him his replacement. When the food came, Lucas said "*Forgetting something?*" with the snotty attitude of a thirteen-year-old. The waitress's face reddened. She apologized profusely and had our meal comped. Lucas spent the whole dinner complaining about our free food, about the staff and the poor management, his bitching and moaning only stopping during the moments he swallowed.

I was repulsed by him on a cellular level: Every part of my body down to each mitochondrion coiled inward and turned away. *How would Normal Sadie react?* She would walk out, never see this man-baby again. I glanced at the restaurant's door, but it seemed so far, and Lucas had driven. How would I get home without him? Normal Sadie would simply call for a ride, I knew, but I was not her and could never do something so bold.

After dinner, I was quiet. I sat in the car with my arms crossed while Lucas drove me home. Lucas was quiet, too, and I hoped he was reflecting on his ridiculous behavior and would soon apologize. But Lucas said nothing. He pulled into a grocery store parking lot and got out of the car without explanation, slamming the door behind him. I didn't know what I was supposed to do. Should I follow him? Get out and walk home? I did neither, just sat there, suspended in time and space as I waited for him. Ten minutes later, he returned with a bouquet of flowers and an expensive bottle of red wine.

"I know dinner wasn't the best. That waitress really fucked things up," Lucas said, ignoring all of his responsibility in the matter. He got back in the car. "So, let me make it up to you at home." He smiled, and his voice was gentle again. It was like the Lucas at dinner had gone into the store and swapped with a nicer clone of himself, the charming version I'd fallen for at the clinic.

He handed the flowers to me. They were pink and had that soft, sweet smell that flowers do. My heart glowed. I'd never been given flowers before. Lucas cupped the side of my neck, kissing me hard. I kissed him back, his stubble prickling my skin, his thumb caressing my clavicle. Suddenly, all my previous cellular repulsion seemed petty, an overreaction. It's not like he'd punched someone in the face and flipped the table. No. I was the one who'd made a big deal out of nothing.

"Co-dependent," my therapist said when I recapped this experience to her in a session.

I shook my head and explained the raw passion between me and Lucas, the flowers, the great sex, the way he made me feel cherished. I showed her my newest pair of earrings from Lucas: a pair of interlocking hearts.

"Love bombing," the therapist replied.

I stiffened. What kind of dumb, made-up term was that?

"Are you sure that this relationship is healthy for you? Maybe your problem isn't just your childhood trauma at camp," the therapist said, slowly, cautiously. "But Lucas as well."

I scoffed—I'd never heard words so false in my life. Lucas was not my problem. He was my solution. That night at camp, Allie and Blakely's deaths—*that* was my problem. My only problem.

I quit that therapist. I'd intended to find a new one; I'd been seeing various ones all my life since Allie and Blakely died. But as I scrolled through local therapists' profiles online, I realized that now that I had Lucas, I didn't need a therapist anymore. The goal of therapy had been to help me cope with my PTSD and strive toward normal, and I'd achieved it, hadn't I? I had a good job and my dream man, who was teaching me powerlifting, and this new hobby made me feel more confident in my body than I'd ever been. My life was finally going in the right direction. That hour a week in therapy was just another hour I could spend in the gym with Lucas. Since we've been together, I've had no need for therapy.

"I'm sorry, babe," I say to Lucas in the car, my voice sweet. "I think I was just getting a little carsick."

He's disgusting, Damon's voice says in my head. *You should leave him.*

Never. I stroke Lucas's ear, the place he likes best, where his earlobe meets his neck. *I need him.*

You don't. You can be happy without him, Damon says, but his voice is weaker, fading, and it's because I'm right: I have to be with Lucas. I'm no one without him. Nothing.

Lucas's tense muscles soften, his tight grip on the steering wheel loosening. I lean closer to him. "I'm really excited to have a weekend together," I coo in his ear, my lips brushing his neck.

The speedometer slows from 90 mph to 80 mph.

"I love you," I say, bringing the speedometer down to a safe 70 mph.

Chapter 8

2006

Allie, Blakely, and I walked out onto the dock while the other kids sprinted into the lake. I sat on the edge of the dock, the warm wood heating the backs of my legs. Allie and Blakely laid on their stomachs a few feet from me, suntanning, talking about beauty tips they'd recently read in *Seventeen* magazine.

"Bina, do you ever shave your arms?" Allie asked, lifting her sunglasses to squint at me, her eyes scanning my body.

"No, why?"

"Maybe you should." Allie snickered. "Someone might think you escaped from the zoo."

I flinched, glancing at my arms. She was right: Thick black hair sprouted from them, starkly contrasting against my pale skin. My arms were especially beastly compared to Allie's blonde-haired ones. Even Blakely's brown arm hair wasn't nearly as coarse and noticeable as mine. I'd tried lemon juice and even bleach before, but my thick, black body hair refused to be lightened. I tucked my forearms into my armpits, dipping my feet into the water.

Tiny fish swam around my toes, clumps of green algae drifting by. A bug skittered across the water, its long spindly legs propelling it across the lake's surface. How strange that this bug could walk on water while other bugs, like all the bees and dragonflies in the pool at home, drowned so easily. Maybe those bugs were stupid, ungifted. Maybe to those talentless bugs, this water-walking bug was like Jesus.

Something touched my foot. I yanked my feet from the water, realizing I hadn't yet checked myself for cuts. How stupid was I? I knew better. All it took was one tiny crack in my skin and the amoebas and parasites could enter my bloodstream and kill me. *Parasites Within* was my favorite TV show. I had seen every episode, twice. I knew all the ways parasites could infiltrate the human body, all the ways a person could be killed from the inside out, and holding all that knowledge made me feel safe and in control, like I could prevent anything bad from ever happening to me.

In one episode, a man jumped into the lake with a small cut on his knee. The next day, he had a stomachache. The day after that, a fever of 103 degrees. The day after that, he was hospitalized and hooked up to a ventilator, his organs shutting down. By the time the doctors realized he had contracted flesh-eating amoebas from the lake, it was too late. All the doctors could do was stand by and watch as the man slowly died, millions of microscopic mouths chewing him apart.

I ran my hands across my calves and toes and knees, feeling for fissures or weak places in my skin. But what about the other holes in my body? If there's a fish that can swim up a man's penis, then couldn't a bug or hungry amoeba find a path into me any way it wanted? It most definitely could, and that meant there was no way I could get into this lake. I'd been stupid to even dip my toes in.

I laid back on the dock, suntanning beside Allie and Blakely, but still, I felt unsettled, paranoid that something was trying to get me. My leg itched. I shot up onto my feet, smacking my skin in case there was a bug, but there wasn't. Still, the paranoia persisted. A flicker of movement across the lake caught my eye. I squinted to get a better look. Why didn't I bring my sunglasses? I shielded my eyes with my hands.

There, across the narrowest part of the lake was a person standing at the tree line, facing me, possibly even staring right back at me, but it was hard to tell because she wore some sort of big hat with white things sticking out of it. Was it a counselor? But why would a counselor be way over there? I could make out that the person was wearing a knee-length white dress and red gloves, which was strange—it was way too hot for gloves. Maybe she was gardening? But who gardens in a forest in a dress?

I stood at the edge of the dock to get a better look, and now I could tell that the woman wasn't wearing a hat, but a big mask that covered her head. The mask had the horns of a deer, the antlers branching out of her head. One red glove was longer than the other, spreading all the way up her arm. My stomach tightened.

The Mean Ones

Those weren't gloves, I realized, but red stains.

Blood.

Maybe it wasn't that weird at all, though; maybe the woman was a hunter. But the dress raised questions. Slowly the woman started to stand on one foot, like a flamingo, and her head cocked to the side, one ear pointed toward the sky. I started to pivot to ask Blakely what she thought of this weird, bloody, masked woman when Allie's hands were on my back, shoving me. I flailed, trying to catch onto something, but I was already falling.

My bare stomach slapped against the surface of the lake, the abrupt sharpness of it like plunging through glass.

My mouth was still open.

Bitter lake water rushed down my throat and up my nostrils.

I accidentally sucked in a breath and choked, the surge of murky water making my chest cramp, my throat seize. I was a good swimmer, but my panic made me stupid, made me thrash and swallow even more lake water. Allie hadn't even pushed me that hard, yet I'd somehow plunged deep underwater. I kicked and swung my arms, accidentally gulping down more lake in the process. Finally, my head broke the surface.

I coughed, spitting out the muck, sucking in air. My throat felt raw, inflamed. My chest ached and burned. Tears and lake water stung my eyes. How many parasites were making their way through me right now?

Allie cackled, doubling over in a shrill, obnoxious laugh. She laughed so hard she snorted. Now that I could breathe again, my panic shifted to fury. My muscles clenched, my skin growing hot with anger—the water around me could've boiled.

Blakely watched me with pity and told Allie, who was still cackling, to shut up. Allie ignored her. Blakely shoved Allie into the lake—she fell forward with a shriek, belly flopping a few feet from me.

"Now you're even!" Blakely shouted, and I knew she meant well, but that wasn't nearly enough to make this all better. My stomach acid was probably killing the parasites I swallowed, but what about the water I inhaled? The water that got into my ears? In my eyes? I could see them now: the parasites swimming in my eyeball fluid, their tiny mouths latching on.

I swam to the dock ladder, heaving myself out of the water as quickly as possible. My feet slipped on the slimy steps, and I had to ungracefully scramble onto the dock. It occurred to me that Jesse could be out there in the lake, witnessing me in this ugly scrambling-panicked state, but I didn't care. I just needed to shower and get the hell away from Allie.

"Are you okay?" Blakely asked. "Allie didn't mean to hurt you—" She touched my arm. I yanked it back.

"Come swim!" Allie shouted from the water, floating on her back. "Don't be a party pooper!"

I stomped away toward the bathrooms, stealing one glance back across the lake to where I'd seen the woman in the white dress. I expected her to be gone by now, but she was still there, still standing on one foot, her head cocked, her red hands open at her sides. What the hell was wrong with her? I would've asked Blakely what she thought, but I was too angry. All I wanted to do was find Ruth and ask to switch cabins. I cry-laughed at how I'd thought I could get along with Allie and Blakely for two whole weeks. We hadn't even made it one day.

Blakely ran up to me. "Where are you going?"

"To see Ruth. I'm changing cabins." I spat, trying to get the murky taste and gritty texture out of my mouth.

Blakely groaned. "Bina, come on. Don't do that."

I didn't intend to really go through with switching cabins. If I did, then I would have to avoid Allie and Blakely for the rest of camp, and Allie would raise hell. Still, it felt good to let the threat feel real.

I charged ahead toward Ruth's cabin, the ground hard and painful on my bare feet. I came to an abrupt stop. All I had to do was step on a sharp rock or piece of glass, and it would all be over. My skin—my number one immune organ—would be punctured. I leaned forward, scanning the ground for sharp objects.

Blakely yelled for Allie, and a moment later, Allie was catching up to us and Blakely was telling her that I was going to switch cabins.

"*Why*? What's wrong?" Allie asked, her long blonde hair dripping down her shoulders.

"What's wrong?" I scoffed. "You freaking pushed me into the lake! I choked." My voice was hoarse, my throat raw. I sounded like I was about to cry and knew this would make Allie call me a baby. Here it comes: "Whiny, crying, *Baby Bina*."

But instead, Allie said something I never expected to come from her perfect little pink mouth: "I'm sorry." Allie reached out and took my hand. "I thought it was funny, but maybe I shouldn't have pushed you."

I stammered.

"Don't go," Allie said. "We can't be Bee-Bee-and-A without you, Bina." Allie held up her wrist, gesturing at her silver bracelet. Blakely held hers up too.

Reluctantly, I raised mine also. We each had matching silver charm bracelets. The dolphin charm was from the time Blakely went to SeaWorld Orlando and brought them back for us. The heart charm we picked out from Claire's at the mall, where we got the bracelets in the first place. Each bracelet had a small nameplate with our own name engraved, and the last three charms were the letters: *B*, *B*, and *A*.

I smiled at the nickname for our friendship trio. Allie was right: Without me, Blakely and Allie would just be Bee and A. That didn't have a ring to it at all.

"You're always overreacting," Blakely said to me.

"Yeah," Allie added. "It was a push into the lake, not over a cliff."

I flinched. Was I overreacting? In the middle of the lake, there was a giant green floaty with a slide. Boys and girls were taking turns shoving each other off it into the water. Maybe pushing each other into the lake was a normal thing to do, and I was making it into a travesty. According to Allie and Blakely, I was always doing this: always making little things into big things. I looked beyond the floaty to the forest, searching for the woman to point her out this time. But she was gone now, though I had the feeling she was still out there somewhere, watching.

"If you change cabins, it'll literally ruin the whole trip," Allie whined. "Don't go to Ruth, okay? Let's just go back to the dock. I won't push you again, promise." Allie looped her arm through mine. "We can talk about how we should set up your first date with Jesse." A grin spread across Allie's face, and then I was smiling too.

But how many times had Allie apologized to me just to turn around and do the same crappy thing the next day? Too many. I knew I shouldn't trust Allie, but she was so pretty, so skinny, so cool, and without Allie, who was I? No one. Just a lone Bee. And when Allie wanted something, I always gave in.

This was, and always would be my problem: I couldn't say no.

Chapter 9

2023

When we arrive at our destination, the cabin is much larger than I expected. It's not even really a cabin but more of a traditional house: two stories, large windows, an expansive balcony. The wooden exterior is the only part that qualifies it as cabin-like. The tension in my body relaxes; this place is nothing like the small, dingy, death-inviting cabin from my childhood. I bet there's even a hot tub.

"You're sure you don't want me to turn back?" Lucas asks, his voice dripping with his unique brand of sarcasm. It's a test, an invitation for me to start him back up again.

"I'm sure," I say sweetly.

"Good." Lucas puts the car in park. There's still an edge of aggression to his tone, his anger meter hovering around 65 percent.

I can sense Lucas's moods the way a medical alert dog can detect an irregular heartbeat, can sniff out his budding rage like a bloodhound smells cancer cells. I learned this skill growing up with Mom, developed this sixth sense from years of tiptoeing around her feelings. Dad never learned this skill and would obliviously walk into the firing range to get yelled at when it could've been avoided if he'd simply scanned her mood before approaching. But I only needed to experience Mom's rage a couple times to develop my intuition for when to approach and when to hide.

That's why Lucas's "anger issue" (my bad ex-therapist's words, not mine) isn't really an issue: I am in control. I know exactly what to say and how to touch him to keep him calm and happy. Sure, I slipped up during the car ride here, but that's because the trees were crying and screaming and there was a dead deer standing in the middle of the street, talking to me. I lost my footing, got distracted on the open road. No wonder he got mad at me: I was acting like a lunatic. If I were him, I would snap at me too. Now, I'm ready to keep my shit together.

I put my hand on top of Lucas's, leaning over and kissing him. "The place looks perfect," I whisper in his ear, stroking the nape of his neck; his anger depletes to 50 percent. Another kiss with tongue and he's at his healthy baseline of 20 percent.

"You're here!" Heather shouts, rushing down the driveway. She's wearing black leggings tucked into brown boots and a fuzzy red flannel jacket. Her light blonde hair is down, her baby bangs recently trimmed, which makes her big blue eyes seem even bigger.

I get out of the car and hug her, feeling massive in her presence, but in a good way, like I'm She-Hulk. Heather's four inches shorter than me and petite. Her skin and clothes carry the rich, sweet smell of flowers.

"Jasmine?" I ask. I only know this because I regularly hang out in her flower shop on my lunch break. It's right next to our favorite local sandwich place.

"You're right." Heather looks genuinely impressed. "You're practically ready to come work with me at the shop."

I laugh. "I don't know about that."

"I'm so glad you came, Sade." Heather's bubbly voice does the cracking thing when she's excited. "I know it was such short notice. I worried it'd end up just being me and the guys. We didn't make you cancel any plans, right?"

"No, not at all!" I say, trying to sound as happy as Heather. But I don't have the natural bubbliness that she does. When I don't really try to sound happy, people assume I'm sick with something terminal. That's the curse of my dull, deadpan natural tone.

"The place looks amazing," I say, really emphasizing my joy. *You are happy*, I tell myself. *Happy happy happy*. "Have you and Eli been here before?"

"Once with Eli's parents. It'll be nice to have the place all to ourselves this time. Let me show you around." Heather loops her arm around mine, then leads me and Lucas inside.

The interior cabin is even more impressive than the outside: tall vaulted ceilings, the moon visible through a skylight, the furniture wooden and rustic. Above the fireplace, a deer head is mounted on the wall, its horns polished, eyes black and glossy. I quickly turn away from it.

The whole place is very outdoorsy and cabin-themed, but

tasteful. The kitchen appliances are stainless steel, the countertops dark marble. I was right: There's a hot tub on the back deck.

On the couch, Eli sits with his feet propped up on an ottoman. His brunette hair is pulled up into a man bun, his long beard combed.

"Yo!" Eli stands and hugs Lucas, slapping him on the back in the way that men do.

"Yo." I give a friendly wave.

"Hey Sadie," Eli says. "Glad you came out."

"How's work?" Lucas asks. "Raking in the big bucks?"

"*Bro.*" Eli gives Lucas a look. "We're skyrocketing in nonfungible token flappenwireburgs." Or something like that. None of it makes any sense to me. So, I smile and nod, asking myself for the hundredth time what possessed Heather to marry Eli. He's not ugly or anything outwardly repulsive, but there's something distant and bossy about him that rubs me the wrong way. Maybe it's just because half of what he says is stuff about software engineering and investments and cryptocurrency—vague things that I don't understand, and the fact that Eli exists in this nebulous, intangible world threatens me. He's only thirty years old but makes me feel elderly and stupid. I also have a theory that he's a cyborg.

When it's clear that I'm no longer a part of this crypto conversation, I scoot away from Eli and Lucas and set my bag on the kitchen counter, pulling out the protein powder and pancake mix. I open the pantry.

Lining the shelves are boxes of granola bars and vegan mac and cheese. Bleh. My stomach plummets—*are Lucas and I going to starve?* Be deprived of real food all weekend? When the four of us go out to dinner, Eli and Heather never judge me and Lucas for ordering meat, but we've never been their guests for a whole weekend. At least I brought the protein powder. Maybe Lucas can catch us a fish.

As if reading my mind, Eli appears at my side. A cyborg with telepathy powers, perhaps? "Don't worry," Eli says. "We picked up groceries and got some just for you guys. We'll grill out."

"Cool." I don't really need proof, but Eli opens the fridge, gesturing at the contents inside. There's a clear bag of raw burger meat, and beside the bag of bloody red meat is a plastic bag of vegan . . . something. It's supposed to be meat, I guess. But the color is too brown and fleshy, the texture like clay, the "meat" so clearly pretending to be something that it is not.

◎

Outside, the four of us sit on folding chairs around the firepit, drinking IPAs, except Heather, who's drinking homemade bottled kombucha. She can be annoying like that.

It's a full moon, the stars bright and abundant in the night sky. A chill runs over me. I take out my phone and lean against Heather's shoulder, holding the camera up to snap a selfie of us. Heather smiles, then sticks her tongue out. I do the same. My dark hair contrasts against Heather's light blonde. We look cute, our eyes bright and faces glowing in the firelight. These will be good for my Instagram, a way to change up my usual feed of lifting videos and cat pictures.

After ten more selfies with Heather, Eli clears his throat. I bring my phone down.

"How about we have a phone-free weekend?" Eli says from across the fire, his voice oddly serious, like a strict boomer father. My eyes narrow.

Aww, come on, babe," Heather says. "It was just a selfie. It's not like we're going to be texting all weekend." She sticks her leg out, rubbing Eli's knee with her toes.

I recognize this gesture, this act of pacification. It's how I would soothe Lucas if he were nearing an emotional flare-up.

But Eli gives no indication that he's angry. Instead, he continues with calm levelheadedness I can only wish Lucas possessed a fraction of. "This weekend is our chance to return to nature." He gestures around at the trees. "Come on, guys," he says so earnestly, it makes me feel like I should toss my phone in the fire right now. "Why don't we make a pact?"

"I do spend too much time on this thing." Lucas pats his phone in his pocket.

"Just one group picture before we put the phones away?" Heather asks. "To commemorate our first camping trip?"

"Let's do it." Eli gestures for everyone to stand.

It takes some finagling, balancing the phone against a beer bottle on top of the cooler. Heather sets the timer, and we scramble to stand with our arms around each other. The picture comes out grainy, the fire in the background too bright against the night sky, but still, I love it. I'm between Heather and Lucas, and since I mostly use my phone to text Heather and she's here with me all weekend, I suppose I don't really need it.

"Going phone-free will be good for my detox," Heather says. "I'm cleansing all toxins from my body, including Instagram."

"Uh-huh." I resist the urge to tell Heather that detoxing isn't really a thing. As long as she has functioning kidneys and a liver, they should do the job just fine. Lucas takes my hand as I sit back down.

Eli pulls a drawstring bag out from beneath his chair and holds it open. "We can put our phones in here."

My eyes narrow. He's awfully prepared for this, but it's probably been his plan all along to get us to "enjoy" a phone-free weekend.

"We're addicted to Instagram," Eli says as we pass the bag around, dropping our phones in. "Brainwashed by its algorithm and capitalism."

I stare straight ahead, internally rolling my eyes. This is rich coming from the crypto bro.

"What if we could live like this all the time?" Eli gesticulates at the woods. "Just live off the land, taking care of each other? No money, no social media. Just gathering berries and making art. The way humans were meant to be."

I take another drink. Eli preaches environmentalism and dreams of an off-the-grid utopia but drives a Jeep and wears brand-new Nikes made by the tiny hands of impoverished children in sweatshops. Though I do have to admit, if one of us could abandon society and survive in the wild, it probably would be Eli. He's the outdoorsy type and actually uses the kayak on top of his Jeep.

There's an awkward silence, and I realize Eli is looking at me, waiting for me to answer what I'd assumed to be rhetorical postulating.

"Oh, uh, sure," I say. But these are my friends, I should be honest to some extent, right? "Actually, probably not. I would hate having to live outside. I need the comforts of modern technology. Especially AC."

Lucas chuckles. "It's true. Sade can't sleep if it's not sixty-eight degrees."

"Well, we'll see how you feel after some quality time in nature," Eli says.

Another long pause.

"You brought hiking shoes, right?" Heather asks me.

"Yeah. If Metcons count as hiking shoes." I finish the rest of my beer, the warm buzz creeping through me.

"We'll go up the mountain tomorrow," Heather says. "It'll be so fun."

I nod, a horrible image unfolding in my mind: my legs twisted the wrong way after I've fallen off a cliff, my splintered bones protruding through my skin, and I need to call a medical helicopter to come save me. But I have no phone because Eli convinced me I would have higher quality nature time without it. I die a slow agonizing death, all thanks to Eli.

"What if we need the phones?" I ask. "What if we need to call for help?" *What if there's something worse than a hiking accident? What if there are people out here who want to hurt us?*

"I'm not locking them away." Eli laughs, gesturing at the phone bag on the ground. "I'll put the phones on the kitchen counter. So, they'll be right there if we need them. We'll bring one on the hike tomorrow in case of an emergency. The bag is just an accountability thing."

"Oh," I say. Maybe I am being a little paranoid. "Right."

"Don't worry, babe," Lucas says, pulling my hand onto his lap. "There's nothing dangerous out here. Black bears, maybe. But they're more scared of you than you are of them."

"Even if there *were* grizzlies"—Heather wipes a drip of kombucha off her chin with the back of her hand—"Lucas could fight them off!"

"Doubtful," I say. "They weigh six hundred pounds and hold you down while they eat you alive. It's a slow eating, too, like you're being ground to death."

Everyone's quiet, then Lucas speaks, an edge creeping into his voice. "You really don't think I could take a bear?"

"Look, it's not bears that I'm worried about," I blurt, not even realizing what I'm saying. The beer is making me slip up. This is what I get for never drinking. One beer makes me stupid, sloppy.

"Oh?" Eli says. "You guys been watching a lot of horror movies? Heather and I just binged all the *Friday the 13th*s. I guess this would be the ideal place for a serial killer to pick us off. Even with our phones, service is spotty. The next cabin is a mile away. The killer could off me and Luke, then it's just you and Heather fending for yourselves."

Heather snorts. "I'd be in good hands. Sadie could take the killer one-on-one."

"Yeah. At least I would try." There is some uncomfortable truth to this: It's why I take lifting so seriously, why I never want to break my routine. It's not just the mental escape it provides, but the physical security. When I was twelve, I had the strength of Kirkland-brand tissue paper and weighed a hundred pounds.

Now I'm a dense 170 pounds, and it's reassuring knowing that the killer who came for me today would need the power of an Icelandic strongman to take me easily.

"Not if he shoots you with a gun," Eli says.

Or that.

Or some other weapon.

An image of the knife seventeen years ago flashes in my mind. The killer sliced Blakely's throat with such ease, like she wasn't made of connective tissue but something soft, like a ripe avocado. My muscles wouldn't be enough to stop a sharp blade, especially not if the killer came up behind me or got me in my sleep.

"Or if he stabbed us with a knife." *Did I just say that out loud? What am I doing?*

Eli nods solemnly. "You know, there was a case a while ago. Some girls were stabbed to death at summer camp, or so it's believed. The bodies were never found, but there was so much blood."

My mouth turns to cotton.

"The Camp Graywood Mystery," Eli continues.

My heart drums in my chest, like the drums in the mines of Moria. I picture that scene where Gandalf politely moves the skeleton's hand off the crumbling tome and reads about the drums in the deep. I know I should be taking this conversation seriously—Eli is talking about *my* cold case for god sake—but these are the places my mind goes.

Eli holds my gaze.

Drums drums drums.

There's no way he could possibly recognize me. I've dyed and relaxed my hair. Had a growth spurt. Practically grew a whole new body. I don't look anything like I used to, and I've known Eli for two and a half years. He's never let on that he suspects I'm not who I say I am.

But he's still watching me, scanning me with those beady cyborg eyes.

Drums drums drums.

"Oh yeah," Heather chirps. "I watched that Hulu documentary with you."

"You fell asleep halfway!" Eli turns to her.

My blood pressure eases. The drums quiet. Of course Eli's not bringing up the murders because of me—he's a true crime guy. Soon, he'll be explaining how it was JonBenét Ramsey's brother all along.

"Three girls were killed at Graywood, right?" Heather asks.

"Two," I correct.

"You saw the documentary?" Eli asks me.

"Yeah." I did not watch it. I can't bear to watch anything about the case, especially not the cheesy reenactments and Hollywood cash grabs.

In the first year after the murders, there were several requests for me to give candid interviews, to have my own episodes on *Dateline* and *American Crime Story*. A French producer wanted to make a documentary starring me alongside Allie and Blakely's families, but by that point, we couldn't be in the same room together. Their families needed someone to blame, and that person ended up being me. Mom wanted to capitalize on my infamy, but Dad and I wanted to stay out of the media. He and I ended up winning that argument. Thank god. Eli would've figured me out long ago if I'd starred in a 2007 true crime documentary that would've ended up on Hulu by now.

"Ohhh, yeah." Eli scratches his beard. "Because one girl got away."

"Good for her," Heather says.

"The documentary painted her out to be some selfish brat," Eli says. "But I agree with you, Heather. She was smart."

I blink rapidly, itching for a way to change the conversation, but I can't think of anything that doesn't seem like I'm trying too hard.

"Did you guys see that new O.J. documentary?" Lucas asks. My oblivious savior. "You guys think his son did it?"

I open another beer, hoping the alcohol will help me relax, but a few drinks in, my stomach feels pinched and sour, my limbs heavy and uncoordinated. A current of exhaustion rushes over me, the day of work, lifting, driving, and heart drumming finally catching up to me. "I think I'm going to head in," I say, standing.

"You feeling okay?" Heather asks.

"Yeah, I'm good. Just beat."

"I'll come in too." Lucas stands.

"No, babe. It's fine." I place my hand on his chest, telling him through my palm that it's okay, that I want him to stay.

"You sure you're okay?" He brushes a lock of my hair back, frowning at me with concern.

"Yeah. Just a headache."

"There's Tylenol in my bag." He plants a gentle kiss on my forehead. "Love you." He sits back down.

"Love you too. See you guys in the morning."

"Night, Sade," Heather says.

In the cabin, I carry our suitcases down the hall to the guest room. Cold air greets me when I open the door, goose bumps erupting across my skin. The window is open, a breeze from the river blowing in. In the center of the room is a queen-sized bed with a white comforter tucked tightly into the mattress, complete with several fluffy green pillows. A ceiling fan spins slowly above my head. I put our suitcases in the closet, then walk over to the window.

Outside, the river is wide and flowing swiftly, its tiny waves glistening in the moonlight. Then I see something else moving—a person is down there, walking along the shore. She's far away, but I can make out that she's wearing a loose white dress, which is odd for a late-night river walk. The woman stops, her head turning to look at me. Something's covering her face: a mask. A deer mask, white horns branching out of her head. Slowly, her right foot rises off the ground, and something's wrong with her hands.

My stomach knots, my pulse hammering.

I blink and look around for signs that I've entered the Other Place. But the hardwood floor beneath my feet is still hardwood floor and things that were on the right are still on the right. The walls are the same sensible beige they were a moment ago.

No. I step back, clenching my hands. *I'm in the real world.*

So how the hell am I seeing that weird woman from camp again at the edge of the river, standing on one foot, her hands covered in blood?

Chapter 10

2006

"Stay with your buddies and do *not* go off the trail," Ruth said, sounding especially cranky that morning. The sun was scalding, the humidity tortuous. Ruth stood at the edge of the bridge where the hiking path began, wearing a bright green visor and a matching CamelBak. "Make sure you have enough water. And *put on your sunscreen.*"

"Gay," one boy muttered, and I wondered what was gay about not wanting a sunburn. Ruth handed out bottled water while Blakely and Allie sprayed sunscreen on each other's upper backs, their tan skin exposed beneath their spaghetti-strap tanks. The hike was going to be three hours, Ruth explained. A loop through the forest that would lead us back to camp in time for dinner.

"Isn't that him?" Allie nudged me, jutting her chin toward Jesse Pierce, who stood with his friends beneath the shade of a tree.

"Yeah." Butterflies flitted in my stomach.

"Say something to him," Allie ordered.

"Like what?!"

"Hey Jesse!" Allie called. His head turned toward us, and Allie flapped her hand for him to come over, and *oh my god*—he started walking our way.

"Just say something about dragons or whatever," Allie hissed.

He stopped a few feet in front of us, hands in his baggy cargo shorts.

"Hi Jesse," I squeaked.

"Hey." He flipped his side-swept hair out of his eyes. "Sabrina, right?"

He knew my name. Of course he did. We'd had math and history together for the last two years. Still, it meant something.

I grinned. "Yep, that's me."

Jesse scratched his arm, red bumps forming where the mosquitos had bitten him.

Mosquitos carry West Nile virus, which can make you go blind and then you die in slow, feverish agony, I thought, but knew it wasn't my best choice for a pickup line. "So, you like *The Inheritance Cycle*?" I chuckled nervously. "I saw you reading it on the bus."

He smiled, dimples forming on each cheek. "Yeah."

My heart triple backflipped.

"Have you read it?" he asked.

"Just finished *Eldest*. Glaedr is so cool, right?"

"He's the bomb. Did you know they're making a movie of *Eragon*?"

I did, and I had my suspicions it was going to suck. "Yeah. I'm excited." What if Jesse and I could see the movie together? My heart and all the rest of my organs glowed at the thought of such a romantic date, but there was no way Mom would send me to the movies alone with a boy. She'd said before that I couldn't be alone with a boy until I was fifteen.

"We should all go see the movie together," Allie said. "My mom will take us."

My hopes soared. If it was a group thing, then Mom would let me go to the movies. Jesse and I really could have our date. "Yeah." I grinned. "Sounds awesome."

"That'd be tight," Jesse said.

His friends called for him.

"See you around." Jesse waved as he walked away.

"Oh my god!" Blakely squealed. "You guys have a date."

"You'll have to straighten your hair for that, Bina," Allie said.

I could see it now: my hair silky, my lips shimmering from Allie's lip gloss. I could sneak Mom's eyeliner into my bag. Maybe during the movie, Jesse and I could hold hands. Maybe even have our first kiss. An involuntary little shriek escaped me.

"Let's march!" Ruth called out, and we followed her and the other kids over the bridge into the forest, our group trailing at the rear. I fanned myself, the excitement of talking to Jesse and the intense sun cooking me alive. Sweat pooled between my skin and backpack, my thighs sticking to my pants.

"Aren't you burning up?" Allie asked, one eyebrow cocked, her hands on her bony hips. Her legs looked impossibly long in her white short-shorts and she was wearing sandals even though Blakely and I both told her that was a bad idea. Allie's blonde hair was parted to the side, like Jamie Lynn Spears's hair in *Zoey 101*. She was wearing her favorite pink dangly earrings from Claire's. She looked ready for the mall, not a hike through the forest.

"I don't want ticks," I explained. "They latch onto bare skin."

"*Ticks?*" Blakely asked, like she'd never heard the word. She was also wearing shorts, though hers were longer, but still not nearly enough protection from ticks.

I nodded. "They carry Lyme disease, which causes chronic pain, fatigue, rashes, and sometimes the symptoms can last your whole life," I said, quoting the Lyme disease episode from *Parasites Within*.

"That's why we have bug spray, duh," Allie said.

"Plenty of ticks are resistant to that stuff. The best defense is to shield your skin entirely."

Allie rolled her eyes but started inspecting her calves and ankles.

"The mosquitos here carry all sorts of diseases." I worried about Jesse's bug bites again. My own skin itched at the thought of the mosquito's proboscis breaking my skin. That's the word for the part of its mouth that saws through skin, and that's actually the verb scientists use when describing how a mosquito feeds: Mosquitos *saw* through our skin, their serrated maxillae cutting through us like wood.

I thought if I learned everything there was to know about

my fears, then it would make them less scary. But it turned out that wasn't true. Instead, it just made me aware that there was even more to fear than I'd previously thought. The image of a mosquito's hairy demonic head beneath a microscope, words like *"the mandibles hold the human flesh apart while the maxillae saw through the victim's skin"*—it all haunted me. Constantly.

I sprayed more bug repellant on my hands, my neck, my face, all the parts of me that weren't covered by clothing. Allie sprayed more of it on, too, misting her ankles and calves. Blakely checked the backs of her legs, tugging at the edge of her shorts. I felt bad for spreading my paranoia, for making my friends share my same fears.

But then again—they should be scared.

◎

An hour into the hike, Allie needed to pee. We were still at the back of the hiking group, and I really didn't want to stop now—Jesse and his friends were a few yards ahead of us. If I really concentrated, I could catch snippets of their conversation, stuff about Pokémon and Yu-Gi-Oh! On our first date at the movie theater, maybe I could bring my Yu-Gi-Oh! cards, and then after that first date, Jesse and I could get together and start dueling regularly. The thought made me more excited than I'd ever felt about anything else, even Christmas morning.

"I need to pee too," Blakely said.

I probably wouldn't have been so annoyed if I also had to pee, but before the hike, I'd squeezed every last ounce of pee from my body and had been watching my water intake. There was no way

I was going to squat bare-butt in the grass, inviting the bugs to crawl up in me to devour my insides.

"Let's be quick?" I asked, watching Jesse and his friends turn the bend up ahead. If Allie and Blakely peed fast, we could speed-walk and catch up. "I don't need to go," I added. "I can keep watch."

Allie stepped off the trail, her sandals flattening the ferns and dense greenery of the forest floor. I shuddered, imagining all the bugs that could be skittering over her exposed feet. Blakely followed Allie off the trail. They crossed the tree line, shadows creeping over them as the thick canopy eclipsed the sun.

"Don't go too far," I said. "We're not supposed to leave the trail."

"Yes, *Ruth*," Allie said sarcastically. Blakely giggled.

They kept walking deeper into the forest. Blakely stumbled over a branch. "That's far enough!" I shouted. "Stay near the trail."

"I'm not peeing where anyone can see!" Allie shouted back.

"Yeah!" Blakely said. "Just wait there. We don't need you lezzing out on us."

Wow. From Blakely's mouth? She really was becoming an Allie mini-me. I said nothing, watching them disappear behind the trees. When they were out of sight, I flipped them off.

A minute went by. Then another. The chatter from Jesse's group had disappeared, replaced by the calling and chirping of birds and what I assumed to be some sort of massive, blubbery frog. The mechanical hum of insect wings buzzed all around me, making my skin crawl.

What was taking Allie and Blakely so long?

What if something bad had happened to them?

I reminded myself that I overreacted about everything. They were probably pooping, probably trying to identify which leaves were safe to use for wiping. *Or maybe they ditched me.*

Another minute passed.

The chirping and croaking and buzzing grew louder. I shifted my weight side to side, craning my neck to try and see the girls through the trees. A branch snapped to my left—the distinct sound of a foot cracking wood. "Allie?" I asked.

No response.

Probably a deer. But what if it was something worse? A wolf? A bear?

"Stay with your buddies," Ruth had said. "Do not go off the trail."

We'd broken the only rules we'd been given. I shouldn't have let my friends wander off.

What if they hadn't ditched me but were genuinely lost?

Being eaten alive by bugs and bears?

I took a step off the trail into the tree line, placing my feet on Allie's footprints. There was no way I could catch up to Jesse and the rest of the hikers and admit I'd lost Allie and Blakely. It would be better to go into the forest and find them, then we could all run ahead to the group and act like we'd never fallen behind.

I didn't even consider the possibility that I could end up lost too.

Chapter 11

2023

She's not real. I pace back and forth in front of the window. There's no way the same crazy woods lady from Alabama is here in Colorado. *Your mind is projecting images to cope with the trauma*, I chant in my ex-therapist's voice. *PTSD-induced hallucinations are common in victims of violent crimes.*

I shut my eyes, count to ten, then check outside the window. The woman is still there, still standing on one foot with her head cocked to the side. *Fuck!* And now she's doing something with her other hand. I press my forehead to the glass to see better—she's holding a knife, a bone-white knife. And she's pointing it at me.

Fuck no.

I close the curtains and double-check that the window is locked.

She's not real. I'm tired. That's all. So very tired! I take a sleeping pill and crawl into bed, yanking the tucked-in comforter free so I can wrap myself up. I listen for footsteps, for someone breaking in. *But what if she is real?* My mind whirrs. *What if she's here to hurt me?*

Maybe I should ask Lucas to go investigate, but then he'll get suspicious. He'll ask what I'm afraid of and I'll have to explain why this woman is dangerous, and how can I do that without exposing my past? She's probably not even real, and then Lucas would realize that I'm both a liar and deranged.

I watch the fan spin on the ceiling until my eyelids grow heavy. Sleep tugs at my mind, my muscles relaxing. My body feels like it's falling, falling, falling.

Then everything goes dark.

Lucas's loud snoring jolts me awake.

I'm cold, blanket-less, my neck tight and cramping. I reach to take the covers from Lucas and grasp only air. I open my eyes, blinking to adjust to the lack of light. My heart starts pounding.

My feet are cold, and my left foot is resting on something hard. The floor. I'm not in the bed—I'm standing *beside* the bed.

I'm standing on one foot.

One fucking foot.

My head is cocked to the side, so I'm staring sideways at the closet, and I can't straighten it back out. My muscles are frozen, my body immobilized. *What the fuck?* My mouth dries, tears prickling my eyes.

I've never sleepwalked before, never had sleep paralysis. I've sure as hell never found myself standing on one foot like this with my neck bent to the side. Maybe I'm having a stroke. I would prefer that over the alternative, *Which is what exactly?* My heart beats faster.

I suck in a breath, and with all my physical power, I lurch my weight to the side—I tip over, tumbling to the floor, landing on my hip with a loud thump. My bent leg extends, and my neck straightens. *Thank god.* I don't know what I would've done if it hadn't.

Lucas snorts in his sleep, rolling over. I dart back into bed and curl up beside him, blood rushing in my ears.

"It's okay," I whisper to myself, winding up in the blankets. *You're fine, totally fine.* My body feels heavy, my muscles crawling with the strange sensation they get when I take sleeping pills, like my muscle fibers are trying to squirm out from under my skin. I stare up at the ceiling fan, watching the blades spin slowly, the skeletal shadows it casts across the room. *Maybe it's the two beers and the sleeping pill—yes, that has to be it.* That's why I got out of bed and stood on one foot. What a stupid, careless thing to do. The realization calms my nerves. My heart rate begins to slow.

I close my eyes, counting backward from one hundred, willing myself to pass out like a patient about to undergo surgery, but sleep is impossible. My neck aches from being cocked to the side for who knows how long. I roll onto my other side, trying to think happy thoughts, but the bad ones keep creeping in. My mind does the thing it always does when I'm having insomnia: It takes me through my worst memories.

One night, a few weeks after Allie and Blakely died, I curled up by my bedroom door, listening to my parents talk about me.

"Honestly, it's better that Sabrina didn't do anything," Dad said, his confidence making me feel a tiny bit better.

"But to just hide there all night?" Mom said. "And not even try to get help when the sun came up and the danger was gone?"

"Maybe she didn't know the danger was gone—"

"She *fell asleep*, Dave. A few feet from where . . ." Mom let out a shuddering breath. "Her friends were stabbed."

My stomach squirmed. That had happened, yes, but not the way they thought.

"Reporters are constantly calling," Mom continued. "I don't know what to tell them."

"Don't tell them anything," Dad said.

"We have to say something. If not, we look like we're hiding her. You know I read an article speculating that Sabrina might've known the killers? That she might've let them in?"

"Isn't that slander?" Dad asked, his voice rising.

"Libel," Mom corrected. "And I don't know if we can do anything because they didn't use her name, but of course everyone in town knows who we fucking are!" Mom slammed the kitchen cabinet.

"Calm down," Dad said. "Bina's sleeping."

"Why did she have to tell the police that she was mad at Allie and Blakely? Why did she have to act that way at the press conference? Why did she—"

"She's just a little kid," Dad defended me.

I ran my hands over my face. I really did screw up at the press conference.

"She's twelve." Mom sniffled. "Not five. You know I can't even go to the store without people gawking? How long until someone paints 'Satanists' on the house again? I've practically been banished from the golf course—Scarlett knows everyone there. She acts like Sabrina killed Allie with her own hands."

I swallowed. Allie's mom had sent letters threatening to "give me what I deserved." Mom threw them away, but like the other hate mail, I fished them out of the trash. And the letters were nothing compared to the hate I got from Allie's little sister at school. I didn't even tell Mom about the dead garter snake I'd found in my locker earlier that day, how it was infested with ants, the sour, rotten smell that had seeped into all my books. I didn't think I'd be able to use my locker, or any of the stuff that was in it, ever again.

"Just ignore them," Dad said to Mom, and even I knew his advice was impossible to take.

"Why couldn't she have just tried to get help?" Mom sobbed.

"It could've gotten her hurt." He hesitated. "Or killed."

"But at least—" Mom started, then paused.

My chest tightened, and just when it seemed like Mom's words might be too much for me to bear, I felt cold, invisible arms embrace me. The light purple walls of my room blackened, red veins pulsing through newly formed fissures. My bed, rats, and dresser had switched to the other side of the room. My heart rate spiked, but the cool touch of a finger brushed a tear off my cheek, and it made my pulse slow.

"At least *what*?" Dad said, his tone unusually harsh. "You're really going to go there?"

The invisible arms around me tightened. *Don't listen to them,*

Damon said. *One day, all the pain will be worth it.*

I didn't really believe him, but his words were comforting. I waited for Mom's response, which never came. But I knew the words she was thinking.

At least she could've died a hero.

Chapter 12

2006

I stepped off the trail and into the forest. Beneath the canopy of trees, it was several degrees cooler. Darker. My sweaty clothes became refreshing against my skin, and then I was a little too cold, a chill shivering down my back.

"Allie?" I shouted. "Blakely?"

A bird called back, a whooping caw that was quickly mimicked by a dozen others. I studied the ground. Blakely and Allie's footprints continued forward, then drifted to the right. I followed them, thinking of what I would say once I found the girls. *This isn't funny, guys! All you had to do was stay near the trail!*

And then one of my sprawling daydreams consumed my thoughts: I see myself stumbling upon Allie and Blakely, who are huddled on the forest floor, lost and crying. A bird has pecked Allie's earrings away, shredded her earlobes. I take Allie and Blakely by the hands and lead them back to camp where Ruth applauds me for being a good camp buddy and rule follower, for saving the day. Allie's ears are taped back together, but she's forever less pretty and humbled and she's nicer to me, too, because I saved her. At dinner, Ruth announces my feat to the whole camp, and Jesse hears about my heroism—yes, he hears and is in awe. He comes up to me and says, "You're so cool, Sabrina. And so hot." We go outside and there is a talking dragon who asks us to climb aboard, and Jesse and I get on its back and off we go, holding each other as we're carried by the dragon's massive flapping wings, and atop the dragon's back, in the sky, Jesse and I have our first kiss.

I yelped when I walked into a prickly bush, the sudden pain of thorny leaves against my hands interrupting my daydream. The grin fell from my face. I inspected myself for insects, making sure none had hopped off the bush onto me. I searched the ground for the footsteps I'd been following, but they were gone. I'd been so lost in my thoughts, I lost the trail. *Damn it.*

I turned to the left, looking for the way back to the hiking path, but all around me were trees, dense bushes, and mossy boulders. Every direction looked the same. My chest tightened. I inhaled, exhaled, listening for voices, for Allie's shrill laugh, for anything that would lead me in the right direction. And then I heard the faint trickle of water. A river had to be nearby, and water always led to civilization. Dad told me that once when we went camping.

Dad was always teaching me useful things like how to tie a bowline knot and figure out which direction I was going based on where the sun was in the sky. I wondered if that's why Allie was such a bitch: She didn't have a dad. But Susie Thompson in our class didn't have a dad, either, and she was nice and invited everyone over for her birthday, even the boy whose breath stank like the sludgy stuff that came out of our broken garbage disposal. I couldn't imagine her ever shit talking about anyone. But Susie's dad died in a car accident while Allie's dad left to go be with another woman who he also apparently had a whole secret family with, and maybe it wasn't just about not having a dad but *how* you lost your dad that made the difference between a mean girl and a nice girl.

I kept following the sound of water and eventually found a clear stream flowing across rocks and fallen branches, small fish swimming up the current. And then I saw a sign of hope—a footprint in the mud. Except it was too big to be Allie's or Blakely's. Maybe it was a counselor's, but then I remembered that weird woman with the mask and bloody hands by the lake. There were other people in these woods, and, yes, that woman's hands had been bloody, but that didn't necessarily mean she was dangerous. Maybe she could help me find my friends.

"Hello?" I called.

A voice murmured to my left, the words indescribable, the tone low and deep. I pivoted toward the sound but didn't see anyone.

"Is someone there?" I shouted, cupping my hands around my mouth.

This time the voice spoke to my right, and someone responded from up ahead, the voices echoing through the trees, the words too quiet for me to understand.

A large shadow moved behind a tree. I lurched in that direction, but when I looked behind the trunk, no one was there. More voices spoke through the woods, some high-pitched and feminine, some deep and masculine, but none of the words were intelligible. They all sounded wrong, like English spoken backward. Who was out here in the woods speaking like that?

Goose bumps spread across my skin.

"Allie!?" I shouted. "It's not funny anymore!" I was sure that the weird voices were not Allie's, but I had to say something, had to disrupt the strange whispering. And I had to get out of there.

I walked quickly along the stream, ignoring the hushed voices all around me. Some of the voices grew clearer, louder, more urgent, and in between backward meaningless phrases, there were a few words that I did recognize.

Girl.

Meat.

Hungry.

So hungry.

I covered my ears and kept running, accidentally stepping into the stream, soaking my feet. I sprinted ahead. My sides cramped. My calves burned, my wet socks rubbing the skin of my feet raw. And then I saw a massive tree ahead, taller and thicker than all the rest. It looked like an ancient, wise tree, the kind that would start speaking to me in a fantasy story and give me a quest.

When I got to the tree, I uncovered my ears. The voices were gone, replaced with normal forest sounds: croaking frogs and chirping birds. I was so tired I wanted to lean my weight against this big tree, but there was probably a whole ecosystem of flesh-eating parasites living on it. I stepped closer, inspecting the bark to see how infested it was, and that's when I noticed the gashes in the wood. They didn't seem natural but like they'd been carved by a knife.

I took a step back and realized the gashes were in the shape of a spiral curling around the tree. I followed the pattern, entranced. The spiral went all the way up the tree and tapered off at the bottom, where there was a hole dug into the trunk. Something light brown and hairy was sticking out of it. I grabbed a stick and nudged the hairy thing free, and it tumbled out onto the forest floor.

For a moment, I wasn't sure what I was looking at, but it seemed to be some sort of toy. I turned it to the side, and then I could tell that the toy had a head and a body. It was a doll: a doll made of long light-brown hair, wound tightly with twine into the shape of two arms, two legs, and a round head. The doll was about the size of my foot and strangely beautiful. Creepy, yes, but well-made, artistic.

My stomach dropped. In this lighting, the hair color could have been Blakely's. What if some crazy woods person shaved Blakely's head and made this doll? I turned around, paranoid that someone—or something—might be sneaking up on me. But I was alone.

I bent down and snatched up the doll quickly, without even thinking about all the lice and spiders that were probably living in it. But I needed a closer look, needed to see if it felt like Blakely's hair.

The texture was coarse, coated with gel or some product that helped the hair hold its doll shape, and I could see now that it didn't have the reddish tint of Blakely's auburn hair. Some of my anxiety soothed. I gave the doll a light squeeze and felt something hard in the center. I spread the hair apart and let out a small scream, dropping the doll.

In the center were several teeth, yellowed with plaque, the roots caked in dried blood.

Chapter 13

2023

In the morning, Heather and I sit on the rustic wooden barstools at the kitchen counter.

"Sleep okay?" she asks.

I shrug. I'm on my second cup of coffee and am halfway through a blueberry protein pancake. My neck's still stiff and my eyes are baggy and dry from last night's lack of sleep, but Heather looks great, her blue eyes bright and shiny, her light blonde hair up in a messy bun. She's wearing the ugly green sweater we picked out on one of our recent thrifting days. It's a light, mossy green and obnoxiously fuzzy. When Heather found it, she held it up and said, "Looks like someone poached the Grinch and made him into a sweater. I *must* have it."

I smile at the memory.

"Something funny?" Heather asks.

"Just remembering when you bought that sweater."

"It's so comfy." She rubs the sleeves. "Eli hates it. He says it smells bad. I told him that's because it's hard to wash the Grinch out of it."

I laugh, almost choking on my coffee. Heather and I both love things that are so ugly they're cute and so bad they're good, like the movie *Samurai Cop*, or Pickles, Heather's dog who recently passed. He was a three-legged long-haired Chihuahua who had a stroke, so his tongue perpetually hung out of his mouth like an old dried-out piece of bacon. She got him like that off Craigslist. Eli was not happy about the dog at first, especially the part where his tongue had to be moisturized daily with olive oil. But Heather didn't care. She just does what she wants whether he approves or not, and part of me admires that, even envies how freeing that must be. And Eli always warms up to her choices in the end.

"What's so funny?" Eli asks, walking past us to the coffee pot.

"We're talking about my Grinch sweater," Heather says.

Eli wrinkles his nose, pouring coffee into a thermos.

Lucas comes up behind me, kissing my cheek. "Sleep okay, babe?" He massages my neck and I groan, leaning back into him.

"Not bad."

Lucas thumbs a knot between my shoulder blades.

"So, what's the plan for today?" Heather asks Eli.

Eli stirs a sugar packet into his coffee. "I'm thinking we check out the local cave. It's a short hike there."

"That sounds cool." Lucas gives my traps one final squeeze, then walks around the kitchen counter to the cabinets.

How can Eli and Heather want to go to the cave? Have they never seen *The Descent*? "But it's such a nice day." I gesture outside. "Why don't we hang out in the sun?"

"Sadie has a point." Lucas gives me an affirming smile, which I reciprocate.

"We'll just check it out for a little bit." Eli takes a sip of coffee. "It's not far, and then we can go on a longer hike afterward. The cave's on the way to the trail we're planning to hike anyway. Sound good?"

"Actually, yeah. I'm down," Lucas says.

My hopes fall.

"Maybe Sadie doesn't want to go to the cave," Heather offers. "And that's okay." She gives me a soft smile.

I smile back, wondering if now is the time to put my foot down and say no to the cave. But Normal Sadie would not be afraid of a cave. Normal Sadie would be down for anything.

"It's cool," I say. "Let's go."

◎

When we're twenty minutes into our hike to the cave, it occurs to me that bats live in caves, and bats give you rabies, and rabies is fifth on my list of the top-five worst ways to die. The rest of the list goes like this: drowning; being stung to death by a swarm of wasps; burning to death; getting stuck upside down in a tight crevice with the blood rushing to my head, slowly starving and suffocating, and when I pee the pee trickles over my body and my face, and eventually I die, and when my body is found, the hikers say *Look at this dumb bitch who got herself stuck upside down.*

I speed up my walking pace, catching up to Heather, Eli, and Lucas, who are a couple yards ahead of me. "Did you know that rabies is one of the worst ways to die?"

"Yeah," Lucas responds. "Why? You scared of bats in the cave?"

"Kind of." I look to Heather for reassurance. She holds my gaze, listening to what else I have to say. "It's pretty common to not feel the bite of a bat," I add. "So, you could get rabies and not even know until you start having symptoms and by then it's too late. You're already going to die."

"Rabies is *extremely* rare, babe." Lucas takes my hand. "I'm pretty sure there have only been a couple cases in the US in the last decade."

I wish I had my phone to look up the statistics; I'm sure it's more than that. At least a couple cases per state. "I think it's actually—"

"I'm inclined to believe the *doctor* on this one," Eli says, cutting me off.

I feel that insult in my gut, but he's right. I'm not a real doctor like Lucas. The only facts I know about the world are from community college, Reddit, and the handful of documentaries I've watched on Amazon Prime.

Lucas's palm heats in mine, his anger meter rising. "Hey," he says in his tough-guy voice, "Sadie's smarter than I am. Really." He stops walking and drops my hand. His shoulders and traps inflate.

I don't want Lucas to go into rage mode here in the middle of a forest trail, but I have to admit there's something attractive about this animalistic response out in the wilderness. It feels right: This is the environment for this sort of reaction, not a restaurant or the mall or the Starbucks parking lot. Part of me would love for Lucas to punch Eli in the face, to punch him so hard he knocks Eli's cyborg head off his shoulders and reveals the wiring beneath, white milky substance spraying everywhere like Ash in *Alien*.

"Eli, stop being a dick," Heather says. "If Sadie doesn't want to go caving because she's scared of rabies or because she just doesn't want to, then she doesn't have to." Heather doubles back to walk beside me. "I'm with Sadie."

My heart swells. I've never had this sort of female camaraderie before, never had a girlfriend (since Blakely) who takes my side. When Lucas sides with me, it feels expected, like it's part of his role as my boyfriend. This female friendship is special, a real choice. It makes me wish we could get into spats more often just so Heather could be on my team.

Eli smacks a fly off his arm. "I didn't mean it like that." He frowns. "But I can see how that sounded. Sorry, Sadie."

I shrug. "It's cool." I turn to Lucas, waiting to see if his anger is going to sustain or drop off. If this were anyone else, Lucas would stay mad and re-escalate the situation, but Eli is his friend, so Lucas de-puffs.

Lucas puts his arm around me. "I won't let the bats get you." He smooches my forehead and I purr.

We walk down the concrete stairs of the cave. The stairs themselves soothe some of my anxiety: This isn't some scary, uncharted

Descent cave. This is a tourist cave, exposed and well-lit with a manmade staircase for easy entry and escape. There are no bats or spiders or crevices to fall into and get trapped upside down in (that I can see). A few other hikers are in here, taking pictures. A skinny white woman sits on a rock, fanning herself. She has long platinum hair twisted into tight locs, which sure is a *choice*. We make eye contact, a bemused expression on her face, and I realize I've been staring. I quickly turn away.

Lucas and Eli take off farther into the cave to go look at the stalactites, and I catch something about "Batman's cave." It's endearing how out here in the wild, these men in their thirties revert to boyhood.

"I'll talk to Eli later," Heather says quietly to me. "He doesn't realize it when he's being an asshole. And I think he's a little threatened by you, honestly. Look at how buff you've gotten." Heather squeezes my arm. I hadn't even considered that Eli could be the one who's threatened by *me* and not the other way around, but the thought is empowering. And it is true that putting on muscle has made people, men especially, see me differently.

"You're looking good too," I say to Heather, and I mean it. CrossFit has made her strong and lean. I can see her traps and delts now that she's changed out of the Grinch sweater and put on a neon-green racerback tank top. She flexes, showing off her bicep, and I give it a little squeeze.

"Jacked," I say. It's different when women put on arm muscle, more admirable. Women have to work at it twice as hard as men. And I wonder why this kind of female friendship where we empower and confide in each other instead of backstab and shit talk had to take me this long to find. Why can't it start like this in girlhood?

I turn to see what the guys are doing. They're wandering deeper into the cave, laughing, bits of their conversation about DC Comics echoing. Heather and I follow them, stepping carefully as the ground becomes slick the farther we go. A stream from outside flows down the cave, clear water rippling over mossy stones. I catch up to Lucas, grabbing his arm to steady myself. The stream continues down into the cave, where it eventually disappears over a ledge. The distant sound of a waterfall reverberates across the rock walls.

Lucas says something to me, but his voice is muffled. I nod absentmindedly. There's a mist hovering where the stream ends and the waterfall begins. A whisper drifts up from the depths of the cave, a low, seductive voice speaking to me, so faint I can't hear the words, but deep in my chest, I know the voice is calling to me.

Without realizing what I'm doing, I start following the sound, my legs carrying me toward the darkest part of the cave. I leave Lucas, Eli, and Heather behind. They don't seem to notice. I'm glad.

There's something at the bottom of the waterfall.

Something I'm supposed to see.

The waterfall grows louder as I get nearer, the water crashing against the rocks below. It sounds like it's a long, long way down.

The light behind me fades. The gnarled stalactites hanging from the ceiling lengthen and curl inward, like large bony hands reaching for me. The stream abruptly stops, like someone has pressed pause on the world, and slowly, the water starts to flow backward, running upward instead of down. The stream's clear water is now a soft, misty blue.

This must be the Other Place, but I've never seen it like this before. Beautiful, almost fantastical.

Normally, these types of visions happen inside my own apartment, and it's gory and unsettling. Here, the Other Place feels natural, like this version of the cave is the true version and the bland real-world version that everyone else sees is the fake one.

Come here, Damon says, his words echoing across the walls of the cave. His deep, husky voice sends a pleasant shiver across my skin.

Come home. My hair gusts back like his breath is on me. A cold, invisible hand caresses the small of my back. My nipples harden.

I turn to see if Heather, Eli, and Lucas are noticing anything, but no, they're chatting several yards away, unaware of all the changes, oblivious to Damon's voice. He sounds like he's speaking from the depths of the cave, his words carried up to me by the stream. *You can be happy here.*

With me.

I take another step toward the ledge.

A few feet ahead, the rocky ground disappears into a dark drop-off.

Jump, a small voice in my mind says. I should be afraid, I know, I shouldn't want to go deeper into the cave, definitely should not want to jump to the bottom. But being this close to the ledge feels inexplicably right.

Chilled air swipes my leg. A girl runs past me, translucent and wispy, her hair flowing like she's underwater. The body shape, the wavy hair, the skip in her step—it's Blakely. She sits on the ledge, her back toward me.

My heart rate kicks up, my stomach tightening. I'm not used to seeing Blakely's ghost like I am Allie's. Slowly, Blakely's head turns. Where her eyes should be are gashed-out holes, the jagged empty pits staring back at me. Her lips curve into an open-mouthed smile. She has no teeth, just gums, like she's an old woman in a little girl's body. Black liquid oozes from the gaps in her gums, dripping down her lips and trickling across her chin.

She makes a "follow me" gesture, then jumps over the ledge. I take a step toward where she'd been sitting.

Come be with us, Damon says.

A hand grips my hip, pulling me back. My attention snaps away from the waterfall.

"What are you doing?" Lucas asks, alarmed.

"Huh?" I blink a few times. *What am I doing?* Why am I all the way over here? I look toward the ledge and am hit with unsettling dizziness from being so close to it. The stalactites have shrunken back into place, the stream clear and flowing normally, the dreamy fantastical comfort—gone. I take a few steps away from the ledge and into the safety of the light. "I was just walking around," I say nonchalantly.

"I thought you were the one who was scared of the cave." Lucas smirks. "Now you're exploring it all on your own?"

"I guess it's not so bad after all." I try to pull him back toward the well-lit main chamber. Now that I'm in a regular, grimy cave again, I just want to be back with Heather and the other tourists.

"Wait," Lucas says, "I like it here." He grips my butt, holding me in place. "It's cozy. Private." He kisses my neck.

I try to focus on Lucas's voice and touch, but my eyes keep pulling back to that ledge. We're still too close to it: I'm hit with the irrational urge to sprint for it, to jump and follow Blakely, to go try to find Damon. I'm paranoid that if I keep looking at the ledge, the intrusive thoughts will get to me, and soon I'll be flinging myself into the abyss. I kiss Lucas, wrapping my arms around him and pivoting our bodies so I'm facing away from the waterfall ledge. Once it's out of my sight, I feel better, grounded.

Lucas walks me up against the wall, pressing me against stone. He hooks his hand beneath my knee, hiking my leg up so my thigh rests at his waist. I run my hands across his absurdly muscular back—there are only twenty pairs of muscles in the human back, yet he feels like he has hundreds.

"You look sexy in these shorts," he says.

"You look sexy in these joggers." I grip his firm butt.

I want you so bad, Damon's voice whispers in my head. *You should be mine.* Chilly fingertips brush my cheeks, chest, the space between my shoulder blades.

I let out a small moan, pushing my tongue against Lucas's, imagining that he is Damon, which is odd because I don't have any conception of what Damon looks like. It's more of a feeling, a feeling of comfort. Of belonging. Of safety. Like putting on a sweater that's warm from the dryer.

"I want to fuck you right here," Lucas whispers in my ear. His hard cock presses against my stomach. He nibbles my bottom lip, his hand sliding up the opening of my shorts.

"I'd like that." The idea of cave sex is hot but impractical. Lucas would have to support my body weight while thrusting at an odd angle; an orgasm on my end would be impossible. Halfway through, he would probably slip out and bend his dick in half, then spend the rest of the trip crying about his broken dick. It's the sort of sex that could only happen in a movie. Still, we make out like it's a possibility, and with Damon's voice still whispering *I want you*, his transcendental hands touching me beneath Lucas's tangible ones, heat courses between my legs, and I almost want to try the cave sex.

Lucas stops kissing me, his brow furrowing. "What the hell is this?" He picks at something behind me. Damon's presence evaporates, all my warm tingly feelings disappearing with him.

"What?" I turn around to see what he's talking about, annoyed that my deranged threesome has stopped.

A wad of blonde hair sticks out from a hole in the cave wall. Lucas pulls at it. Sections of the hair are tied off with twine.

My stomach falls. *No.* Zaps of panic raise my blood pressure.

This can't be happening. Lucas needs to leave that thing alone. But before I can stop him, it tumbles to the floor. A mass of blonde hair, shaped so it has limbs and a head. *A human hair doll.*

He picks it up, frowning. "Weird."

The hair-doll looks exactly like the one from my childhood, except the hair is light blonde.

Just like Allie's hair.

Saliva coats my mouth, bile stinging my throat.

"You think this is from a bird's nest or something?" He drops it onto the floor.

"Uh-huh—" I start to say before throwing up coffee and pancakes.

Chapter 14

2006

I backed away from the hair-doll and teeth, my hands shaking. *Why did I touch it?* It was probably infested with diseases and parasites. I opened my backpack and squirted hand sanitizer onto my palms, the cool gel calming me down as I massaged it between my fingers. Then I took a step toward the teeth to look more closely; it was hard not to, like when you pass a car accident on the freeway and kind of want to see a dead body but also don't. Were these human teeth? And why were they stuffed inside hair and put into a tree, and why was the hair shaped like a doll?

I studied the teeth, turning them over with a stick. There were five. Two looked like front teeth and three were molars. One of the molars had a glint of metal from a filled cavity. Definitely human. My stomach rolled, my anxiety spiking. Something very bad was going on here. But Allie's words repeated in my mind: *"You always make a big thing out of nothing."*

Was this another instance of me overreacting? Maybe this wasn't something sinister at all. Maybe this teeth-filled hair-doll was just some backwoods tooth fairy offering, and I was freaking out over nothing, like the time Allie, Blakely, and I were at Allie's house and the tornado siren went off and Allie and Blakely wanted to ignore it but I made us all go to the basement and stay there and we missed the whole new episode of *The Simple Life*; the tornado never even touched ground. Or the time I ripped a tag off a pillow in Ikea and then I saw the warning label: "Under Penalty of Law, Do Not Remove," and I started panicking, sure that a SWAT team was about to swing through the windows and take me to prison. Nothing happened then either.

My hammering heart settled. This doll was probably like those times where I thought something terrible was going to happen, but nothing ended up happening at all. The gutted doll lay on the ground, the hair disheveled from where I'd pulled it apart to remove the teeth. Now I felt bad that I'd desecrated something sacred. I'd committed vandalism, had potentially ruined some poor kid's chances at appeasing the tooth fairy (tooth demon?).

I used a leaf to pick up the teeth so I wouldn't catch their germs, then I dropped the teeth back into the hair, patted it down with my foot, then used the stick to stuff the whole thing back in its place in the tree. I was a Good Girl, a Polite Girl, a Girl Who Did the Right Thing. This hair-doll was someone's art; it deserved to be treated well.

I still needed to find Allie and Blakely, but the hair-doll had really thrown me off and now I didn't know which way to go. *I just have to keep following the river*, I reminded myself. So, I kept walking.

Walking.

Walking.

My hair stuck to my neck from sweat. My stomach growled. A burning tightness spread up the backs of my legs, my feet blistering from my wet socks.

I passed a series of large boulders, smooth and gray, and out in an open clearing unlike all the rocks I'd seen so far. I stopped. There was something written on the rocks. Maybe I was near the campsite. I moved closer and could see that the rocks were covered in drawings etched with charcoal. Little stick-figure people standing in a circle. It reminded me of the scene in *Ice Age* when Manfred sees the cave wall art and there're stick figures throwing spears at a Mammoth.

Then the stick figures began to move, slowly at first, then with more vigor. The stick figures were all holding something sharp, a knife I supposed, and they jabbed a smaller stick figure, the only one who was knifeless. The smaller stick figure fell over, blood pouring from its neck. A hole opened in the middle of the ground between the stick people, then the stick people dropped to their knees and a larger stick figure with horns floated up out of the hole.

It was the weirdest daydream I'd ever had, and it must've been brought on because of my hunger and stress and memories of *Ice Age*. I rubbed my eyes and the images on the rock were still again. I sighed. *See? Just a daydream.* Then the stick figures started to sway side to side. I leapt back, my heart skipping. If I didn't get out of these woods soon, I was going to lose my mind.

A cracking sound came from behind me. I turned around, hoping it was Allie and Blakely. But it wasn't. Instead, behind a tree a few yards away, there was a big animal, watching me.

A deer. Except it wasn't right.

The deer stood on two legs, like a man. Its legs were long, too long, and instead of hooves, the ends of its front legs extended into black claws, sharp and curled like an eagle's. The deer's abdomen was split open. Flies walked across its exposed ribs. Intestines draped over its lower stomach.

The deer's head was knocked to the side, its neck broken, the notches of its cervical spine exposed. The thing took a step toward me. Its antlers looked weird too—I thought it was because its head was sideways, but now I realized they looked weird because they weren't antlers.

They were human hands.

Skinny, pale human hands growing from the deer's head, broken fingernails reaching out.

My veins chilled from my fingertips to my toes. But there was no way this thing was real—I had to still be trapped in my own daydream that was quickly becoming a day-nightmare. I had to be, *right?*

The deer took another shambling step toward me. Its right leg was mangled, hoof obliterated. Bits of stringy flesh dragged on the ground. It didn't even make sense how it was walking, but it was.

And it was getting closer.

The deer took another limping step. Guts spilled out of its

open abdomen, grisly tubes of intestine splattering to the ground. I closed my eyes. *It's not real. Not real, not real.*

But what if it is? another voice in my head asked. *What if it killed Blakely and Allie and now it's going to kill you?*

I shook my head. "Bina has such a wild imagination," Mom always said about me. "Always reading and watching fantasy movies. You should hear the things she comes up with!" Yes, that's all this was. My imagination.

A snort sounded inches from my face. Heavy, hot breath gusted against my cheeks. The iron scent of blood assaulted my nose, the musty rank of rotting meat, acrid and pungent. I peeked one eye open to see the deer's large shiny black eyes staring at me. Its long eyelashes were stuck together with blood. Flies walked across its wet eyeballs.

Bile burned in the back of my throat. *Not real! Not real!*

I squeezed my eyes shut again, and a moment later, the hot breathing and stench were gone.

"What are you doing here?" a woman said.

My eyes snapped open. There was no deer monster. I checked behind me to make sure it really was gone. I didn't see it anywhere. My quick breathing started to slow. *Just a daydream nightmare. Just a daydream nightmare.*

"Are you alright?" the woman asked, her voice hoarse and raspy. She was a few yards to my right and wore a tattered white dress. She might have been the woman I'd seen across the lake the other day, but I couldn't be sure. "What's wrong?"

"I'm lost." I wiped the tears forming in my eyes. "Have you seen my friends? Two girls?"

She took another step. I wanted to hug her even though she looked like a homeless woman who lived in the woods, probably in a cave since her skin was pale and waxy. She was around my mom's age with deep cheek lines. Her long, greasy black hair fell to her waist. Her overall look reminded me of Gríma Wormtongue from *The Lord of the Rings*. Still, I wasn't scared. She was an adult and a woman. If she were a man, I would be running away. But women were trustworthy, natural caretakers of children. Mom always told me that if a strange man was ever scaring me or I was lost, I just needed to find the closest woman for help. I hadn't yet learned that women could be just as bad as men.

"I haven't seen anyone," Gríma Wormtongue said.

"Did you see…" What should I say? A walking demon deer? No. It had all been in my head. There was no need to bring it up. But then Gríma Wormtongue looked down and sidestepped, a curious expression on her face. My stomach fell, my blood going cold again.

She was avoiding a pile of guts on the ground. The same exact grisly intestines I'd seen fall out of the deer.

Holy shit.

It had been real.

The deer monster really was here.

I started to cry harder.

"Did I see what?" she asked.

"A deer," I sobbed. "But it was all wrong. It walked upright and had hands on its head. I know it sounds crazy but—" I wiped my eyes and noticed that Gríma Wormtongue was smiling, her teeth decaying and jagged.

Now, I wasn't so sure about her. I took a step back.

She clutched her hands together. Her gray eyes flashed with excitement.

"*He's here*," she said.

"What?"

"Go that way," Gríma Wormtongue said, ignoring my question and pointing behind me. "Keep going about a half mile until you see the mossy big boulder by the tree with the roots. You'll find the camp near there."

I nodded. "Thank you," I said, then I ran.

Chapter 15

2023

Lucas leaps back from my vomit on the cave floor. "Watch it!" His face twists with disgust, then softens to concern. "Are you okay?"

I nod, wiping my mouth, keeping my eyes closed. *The hair-doll has nothing to do with the hair-doll from seventeen years ago. The hair-doll has nothing to do with the hair-doll from seventeen years ago*, I tell myself ten more times. There are no teeth in the hair. (I did not check, but I have decided that there are no teeth.) This hair-doll is something made by an odd child or perhaps an artistic bird. The alternative is unfathomable.

The fact that I thought I was reliving the same event from my childhood trauma is just my confirmation bias. My ex-therapist used to say that I'm prone to inventing imaginary things to confirm that my twisted view of the world is correct: That's why

I see and hear things that aren't really there. It's my sick mind. Nothing else.

I open my eyes and give Lucas a soft smile. "I'm good."

He flicks a chunk of pancake off my chin, grimacing. "You don't have a stomach bug, do you?"

"No." I search for a lie. "Breakfast just didn't sit well with me. I feel way better now." I try to sound believable, happy even, but I'm undeniably frazzled, my voice quivering.

"Well, I guess we better leave then," Lucas says, his tone bitter.

"Yeah, let's go." I need to get out of this place, as far away from the hair as possible.

Lucas turns and stomps away from me.

I dump some of my water bottle out onto the vomit, washing it away so another hiker doesn't step in my half-digested breakfast, then I follow Lucas, resisting the urge to look back at the hair-doll. I don't need to see it again—*If I don't look, it's not real*—but my head impulsively swings to look at the thing.

The hair-doll is still on the ground where Lucas left it, but now I realize it doesn't look nearly as doll-like as I thought it had before. Instead of a doll, it might just be a clumpy wad of hair with some limb-like protrusions, probably something from a bird's nest. The hair is a darker shade than Allie's, I'm sure, more strawberry-blonde than platinum. I let out a relieved chuckle. I really had made this out to be something more than it is. Then my eyes pan to the cave ledge again, to the abyss where Blakely's ghost had leapt off into.

Don't leave, Damon says. *That wasn't supposed to be there. I don't want to scare you.*

His voice tugs at something in my chest, but I turn away and quicken my pace to catch up to Lucas and Eli, hopping over the stones near the stream.

My feet slip out from under me on a slick patch. An involuntary yelp escapes me as my ass slams to the ground. My wrists break my fall, palms sliding across slimy moss. A sharp pain shoots through my left hand.

Are you okay? Damon asks.

"Oh my god!" Heather says, her voice making a high-pitched crack. "Are you hurt?"

"I'm good." I stand, inspecting my left hand. A rock is embedded in my palm. I pluck it out, wincing. Blood oozes from the wound, leaking between my fingers. Once, I would've been panicking about infection, but now I'm just annoyed by how this will make holding the barbell painful. It better heal quickly.

Heather gasps when she sees my hand. "Aww, Sade. That looks painful."

I shrug. "It's not bad."

"We need to clean that out." Heather takes her backpack off and riffles through it. Lucas and Eli, who'd been standing by the cave entrance, are now doubling back to check out the commotion.

Heather opens a first aid kit and starts soaking up the blood with gauze. "We need to go back to the cabin where we can wash this."

Lucas groans. "Oh, come on, we were just about to go on the hike."

"It's fine," I say to Heather. "Just put some of that Neosporin on it."

Heather shakes her head. "I'd really rather clean and bandage this properly. You don't know what kind of bacteria is in this stream."

My pulse rises, my old fears threatening to crawl back in. "Okay. But we'll be quick."

The muscles in Lucas's temples flex, a vein pulsing on his forehead. "Why are you so clumsy?"

"I don't know. I just tripped—"

"Exactly. You don't pay attention." Lucas points a finger at me, like he's scolding a dog that's made a mess. "You're always spacing out."

Tears sting my eyes. He's not wrong.

He is wrong, Damon says.

I close my eyes, trying to block out Damon's voice. "It's fine. We'll stop by the cabin, then we can still go on the hike."

Lucas groans, throwing his hands up. "That'll take forever."

I look away from Lucas. I know he doesn't care that much about the hike—he's mad because I didn't get on my knees and suck his dick back when we were in that private corner.

"You two go without us," Heather says, a bossy finality to her tone. I didn't know she could sound like this.

Lucas starts to argue, but Heather gives Eli a look. They hold each other's gaze for a moment, some husband-wife telepathy going on, and then Eli says, "Come on, man. Let them have a girls' afternoon. We'll hike quicker without them."

Lucas shifts his weight, considering.

"We can make it up the whole mountain before dark," Eli adds.

Lucas perks up at this. Without saying a word to me, he runs off with Eli.

Once Lucas is away, I can breathe easier. I love him, I do, but even I can admit that his presence can be oppressive, stifling. It's not his fault, though: His parents spoiled him. If they hadn't given him absolutely everything he wanted as a child, he wouldn't be this way. He'd be able to handle disappointment; he would expect it—even embrace it—like I've learned to.

"You know why Lucas was such a brat right now?" Heather asks.

I flinch at her use of the word *brat*. "Why?"

"Because you were the center of attention and he wasn't. Lucas is only happy when he's the star." Heather looks me in the eyes.

I glance away, her words hitting me in the gut. She doesn't know about his disappointment over the missed cave blowjob, but she's on the right track.

"Frankly," Heather says, "I think he's an asshole."

Well, I think your husband is a robot! I mentally quip back. But I don't say it out loud because Heather's words actually ring true. "Lucas has his moments," I say to the ground. "But he's good to me. He really is." I think of all the flowers, the time he made a sardine birthday cake for the cats, the way he lifts my chin and kisses my forehead when he gets home from work. The man who makes me feel more loved than I've ever felt before is not a bad guy.

You deserve better, Damon says. *He doesn't care about you. Not like I do.*

"Shut up," I mutter under my breath.

"Uh-huh," Heather says with a flat, unconvincing tone. She holds the bloodied gauze, looking around for a trash can, but there isn't one. "Let's get back to the cabin." She folds up my bloodied bandages, putting them into her backpack.

Chapter 16

2006

I ran in the direction Gríma Wormtongue pointed, our odd conversation still fresh in my mind. *Who is "he"?* Why was the woman so excited that "he" was here? Did that woman really live in the woods? I stumbled over an arrangement of small rocks, and quickly righted myself before I twisted my ankle. First, I just had to get out of here, then I could worry about all the weirdness in the woods.

I kept running, ignoring the stitch in my side, the screaming tightness in my calves, the sting of the blisters growing on my heels. Eventually, I arrived at the boulder the woman must've been referencing.

Roots from a tree grew over a massive rock, and the rock itself was green with moss. It looked like something from the set of a

Lord of the Rings movie, the place where Frodo, Sam, Merry, and Pippin hide from the Black Riders. In different circumstances, I might've stopped longer to admire the beauty of it.

Shrill laughter echoed through the trees. Allie's obnoxious voice was unmistakable. Blakely shouted something in response. They were alive. They were okay.

I clenched my fists, heat flaring in my cheeks. What could they possibly be laughing about? For all they knew, I was out here in the woods dying a slow, horrible death, and they were together having a good time.

Those bitches.

I was half tempted to stay out there, to stay so long they would have no choice but to worry and then feel bad and get in trouble for leaving me, and a search party would have to come rescue me, but then I remembered the deer monster and all the bugs and how bad my feet hurt and the grumbling in my stomach. I stomped toward the sound of their voices.

The trees grew thinner, the sun brighter, and a moment later, I popped out into the open and was back on the trail. The trail converged with the campgrounds, and there were Allie and Blakely, standing by some picnic benches with Ruth. Allie had that smug, shit-eating grin on her face that she only wore when she was in trouble. Blakely stared guiltily down at the ground. Ruth's face was red with anger, and she was making frustrated gestures with her hands, then she noticed me. Ruth's face got even redder, her freckles disappearing as her face became one crimson shade.

Ruth stormed toward me. "Where have you been? You had one rule, one! Stay with your friends and do not leave the trail!"

I resisted the urge to point out that it was two rules, not one. And why was I getting chewed out when it was Allie and Blakely who had ditched me? "They went off the trail first." I pointed at the girls. "I was the one looking for *them*." Then my voice cracked and the tears came, the exhaustion and fear and stress of it all hitting me at once.

Ruth's expression softened, her redness decreasing to pink. Blakely gave me a hug. Even Allie looked momentarily apologetic. I wiped my nose on my sleeve.

"When we got back to the trail, you were gone," Blakely said. "We ran ahead to see if you'd moved on without us, but we couldn't find you."

My eyes narrowed. *Liars*. I'd waited so long for them before I went into the forest. But what if they'd gotten turned around and went back to the wrong place on the trail? Maybe it wasn't really their fault.

"What happened out there?" Blakely asked. "How did you get back?"

"A woman pointed me in the right direction. Do people live in the forest?" I asked Ruth. "Because there were drawings and stuff. I found a doll. Handmade."

Ruth cocked her head at me. "Not that I know of." She thought for another moment. "Probably teenagers getting up to no good."

"And there was a deer," I added.

"Duh, there's deer in the forest, Bina," Allie said.

I shook my head. "This one wasn't normal." If I described what I saw, I'd sound crazy, but since there really was a deer monster out there, I had to warn them, right? "It walked upright," I said, staring Allie in the eyes to show her I wasn't kidding. "Its stomach was all open and its guts were hanging out." I shuddered. *It had fingers for antlers.*

"Probably chronic wasting disease," Ruth said.

"Huh?"

"A darn shame. The deer get the disease and start going mad, can survive anything but a gunshot to the head. Hopefully, a hunter will put it out of its misery."

I shuddered. The thought of a crazed, diseased deer was even scarier to me than a demon one, but I didn't think the deer I saw simply had "chronic wasting disease." But without photo evidence or some physical proof, how could I ever convince an adult? Especially one as serious as Ruth?

"Now," Ruth continued, her tone stern again, "you girls get to the dining hall and do *not* break any more rules. You're at one strike." She stuck a finger in the air. "Get two more and you're getting sent home." She walked away.

"You really saw a deer walking upright?" Blakely asked, her eyes wide.

"Yeah, and other things too." I told them about the moving rock drawings and the weird Gríma Wormtongue woman and the hair-doll with the teeth. My voice quivered when I told them about how one molar had a metal filling. "They were definitely human teeth. The whole thing was so scary."

Blakely squinted skeptically.

"You guys believe me, right?" My voice cracked with desperation. I needed them to believe me, to feel how scared I'd been. I needed them to know that there were dangerous things out there in the woods. If they wouldn't believe me, who else would?

Allie stared at me, her arms folded. She snorted. "Yeah, right. You're so full of shit."

I decided I'd never tell them anything important ever again.

Chapter 17

2023

After helping wash and bandage my hand, Heather pours us each a glass of white wine.

"No kombucha?" I ask.

"I'm a day drinker." She smirks, carrying the glasses to the living room.

I follow, sitting beside her on the couch.

Heather hands me a glass, turning so she's facing me, one foot folded across her lap. "How are things between you and Lucas?"

I recognize this tone: It's the therapist one, the "how are things *really*" tone. "Great," I say. "I mean they really are great—the cave thing was just a fluke."

Heather blinks at me, sipping wine.

I wait for her to say something, but she just looks at me with those bright blue eyes, letting me marinate in silence. I look away, pretending to be interested in the artwork in the room. The deer head above the fireplace stares back at me, its glossy black eyes too real. I break eye contact with it, searching for something else to focus on. Generic paintings of robins and trees hang on the wall, the kind of mass-produced art used to fill hotel rooms. I clear my throat. "What about you and Eli?"

"We're good." Her eyes flit to her wedding ring, and a small smile forms on her lips. "We get each other."

Why can't Lucas propose to me already? We're coming up on three years. *Maybe I should've given him that cave blowjob!* I cringe at myself. Normal Sadie, Strong Sadie, would know that she shouldn't have to give a cave blowjob to deserve a proposal. But I'm not really Strong, Normal Sadie, am I?

"Why do you want to be with Lucas?" Heather asks.

I stiffen. Why would Heather even ask me that? "I love him. He makes me happy."

"Does he really?"

"Yes." It's true: I've never been happier, have never felt the level of peace or normalcy I've managed to achieve with Lucas in my life. But Heather wouldn't understand that.

"You've never had any doubts?"

I chuckle nervously and take a drink. I've had doubts, sure, but doesn't everyone? The first Christmas Lucas and I were together, we spent it with his family, like we have every year since we started dating and probably will for the rest of our lives. Sitting on the oversized white couch in his parents' sparse, bland McMansion, I wondered if I could really feel at home there. I knew

I didn't *have* to adopt Lucas's parents as my own, but considering my dad's death and my estrangement from my own mom, some degree of closeness with his parents was inevitable. Their place would always be the receptacle for holidays, birthdays, any meaningful celebration. It was too big, soulless, everything white but for a few beige pieces of furniture.

When it was time to open presents, his mother gifted me a Tolera essential oil diffuser with lavender and peppermint oils that she claimed would soothe muscle pain better than any massage or drug. I recognized the brand: Tolera was an MLM that sold snake oil products. In order to make any money, you had to recruit people who had to recruit more people who had to recruit even more people. A pyramid scheme with half an extra step.

"These are great!" Lucas held the peppermint oil to his nose.

His mother beamed. "Now, Sadie," she turned to me, "rub the lavender on your feet before bed and you'll have the best sleep of your life. The oil works on a cellular level, trust me."

I smiled and nodded, wondering what the hell she thought "cellular level" meant.

"Thanks, Mom." Lucas gave her a peck on the cheek.

My stomach pitted. I'd thought Lucas was so smart; how could he be happy that I'd received expensive scented water? How could he let his mother be a part of a pyramid scheme? But it wasn't my place to question him or his mother.

Later, when it was just the two of us in Lucas's old childhood-bedroom-turned-guest room, Lucas confided that he didn't really believe in the oils. He explained how his mom had lost thousands and thousands of dollars to Tolera. "She's in denial about the money loss, and my dad just keeps funding her oil 'business' to keep her happy. I think if she didn't have her essential oils, then she wouldn't have any purpose. So, we all just pretend that her oils really do help us."

I nuzzled my head against Lucas's chest. Now that I knew these affluent, seemingly perfect people had their own lies, their own secret identities, I felt more comfortable. We were openly admitting that sometimes it was better to conceal the truth, to put up a front and live in that denial. Only in our lies could we thrive.

"I mean, I've had the occasional doubt, sure," I answer Heather's question, taking another drink of wine.

Heather's eyebrows perk.

"But it's never been anything significant." I try to sharpen my voice to sound confident. "Have *you* had doubts about Eli?"

Heather shrugs. "We've had our spats."

"Tell me again how long you two have been together?" I ask, eager to shift the conversation away from me and Lucas.

"Twenty-four years," Heather says.

"Huh?"

She shakes her head, chuckling. Her cheeks pinken. "I meant to say we got married when we were twenty-four. We've been married . . ." She glances up. "Six years?"

"Oh," I say, trying not to seem jealous. I know twenty-nine is technically still young, but sitting here with my friend who got married at twenty-four, I feel like an ancient spinster.

"But we've known each other since childhood," Heather continues.

"Really?" That's weird, and why didn't I know that before? I'd been pretty sure they were high school sweethearts but *elementary school* sweethearts?

"Our families were close," Heather adds, reading my reaction. "That's how it is in Witness families." She shrugs.

"Eli was a Witness too?" Heather doesn't talk much about her Jehovah's Witnesses past. She's only made vague references about it and mirthless jokes about how she spent her childhood summers prepping for the end of the world while other kids went to the movies and had birthday parties. From the brief, forced-funny way she talks about it, I sense there's a lot of trauma there.

Heather nods. "He doesn't like to talk about it."

I didn't know Eli was also a Witness, never would've guessed it based on the modern tech bro he's become, but I have heard that when people are raised in oppressive ideologies, they often embrace the opposite culture once they're free, like Catholic school girls who become porn stars.

"You and Lucas are coming up on three years, right?" Heather asks.

"Yep. This July."

Heather takes another drink, watching me for a long moment. "Do you ever wonder what your life would be like if you could be free of Lucas?"

I pause, a tightness creeping through my chest. What kind of question is that? And what's with that phrasing: *free* of Lucas? It sounds sinister, like he could disappear or die. I don't like it at all.

"No," I say definitively. They're the truest words I've spoken: I never want to be free of Lucas. He's all I have. He's all I want. I take a gulp of wine, the bittersweetness sharp as it goes down my throat.

"Who are you without Lucas, Sadie?" Heather leans closer to me, her eyes searching mine.

"I don't know." I look up at the vaulted wooden ceiling, at the sparse, thin clouds through the skylight. Why can't we just watch a so-bad-it's-good movie or talk about her catty bridezilla clients and gossip about her neighbor's Botox, like normal? "No one, I guess. I'm Lucas's girlfriend, hopefully, soon, his wife. That's me." Another gulp of wine. "I'm happy with that."

Heather shakes her head. "But that's not you. I need you to see that, Sadie. You're special."

"Why?" I scoff, taking another drink. "Because I'm good at lifting weights?" *Because I survived the camp murders?*

"There's so much for you in life." Heather gives me a pitiful look. "I don't want you to feel like Lucas is all there is."

But he *is* all there is. How can she tell me he's not? I don't want to keep talking about this. "I need a nap," I say, which isn't a lie. I set the wine glass on the table and quickly walk to the bathroom before Heather can stop me.

I lock the bathroom door and lean against the counter, my temples and hand throbbing. *Special.* I scoff. Where (and when) I grew up, *special* was just another word for mentally deranged, and that part about me probably is true. I search Heather's toiletry bag, digging through her face moisturizers and toners, looking for a bottle of ibuprofen. I feel a pinch of guilt over my nonexistent skincare routine. Why don't I own any products like this? Because getting older and wrinkly always seemed like a distant concept, but it's right around the corner. Hell, it's here. I lock eyes with myself in the mirror, noting the sunspots on my cheeks, the tiny lines in the corners of my eyelids. Heather's skin is flawless; I need to get it together and start using this stuff. I make a mental note of which brand her products are, take two ibuprofens, then splash water on my face, the brisk cold soothing my headache.

When I reach to grab the towel to my right, I touch only air. The floral towel that was there moments ago is now hanging to my left, and instead of the soft pink flowers that'd been stitched into the fabric, they're now brown and wilting. The dead petals move, falling down the towel, disappearing into the counter. It looks so real, I reach out to touch the towel, expecting to feel fabric, but a dry, crispy flower petal flakes off and turns to dust in my hands. I laugh. I'm absolutely insane.

The white-and-beige marble countertop I'm leaning against has darkened to a grayish black, the lines in the countertop red, pulsing like veins. My reflection looks different too: My brown eyes are practically glowing. My hair flows around me with unnatural volume, like I'm underwater. My skin is smooth, blemish-free. Ageless.

I close my eyes, counting to ten. Soon, the Other Place will disappear, but I have to admit, there's something nice about being here, something soothing. The tension in my head from Heather's questioning eases. My pulse slows back to its usual resting rate. This is *my* place, *my* world, where I'm safe from Heather's or anyone else's judgment. I want to be Normal Sadie, but I'm not sure I can let go of the Other Place, not sure I physically can.

Not sure I even want to.

That thought hits me with a wave of guilt. *Normal Sadie does not have an Other Place.* That's an aspect of my relationship with Lucas that Heather can never understand: When he is around, the Other Place is less frequent. In fact, I've been seeing the Other Place too much out here in the forest, probably because the setting is too reminiscent of my childhood. Just forty-eight more hours, and I can be home, back in my safe, busy routine.

A hand grips my shoulder, the touch cold and strong. I look behind me even though I know no one will be there. Still, a small guilty part of me hopes that he is real, that one day, I will see him. I turn back to the counter and feel cool, invisible fingers interlocking with my own.

Damon whispers in my ear, his words raising the hairs on my neck. *She's right.*

Chapter 18

2006

I tried to stay mad at Allie and Blakely for not believing me about the deer monster and the hair-doll and teeth. *And for ditching me in the woods in the first place!* I really did. But my anger stamina lasted until we were in the cafeteria and I was holding my tray of spaghetti and green beans and I realized I had two options: stay mad and sit alone, or admit defeat and sit with Allie and Blakely.

Blakely sat at a table in the corner of the dining hall, her backpack saving the seat beside her for Allie. I joined her silently. A few minutes later, Allie arrived with a tray of food, claiming she had to run back to the cabin for something. She whispered to Blakely, both of them smiling in their smug, stupid way. I rolled my eyes, waiting for them to tease me more about the demon deer or how much food was on my plate, but Blakely started talking about the Disney World vacation her family had planned for next Christmas. A flicker of envy crossed Allie's face. Ever since her dad left, she didn't get to go on family vacations anymore.

The conversation about Disney World petered out. Blakely ate her lime Jell-O before her spaghetti because she was weird like that. Allie drank two glasses of water before touching any of her food because it "helped her eat less." I was the one in our group who ate normally, and I was proud of that.

"Does your family ever do trips for Christmas?" Blakely asked me.

I shrugged. Last year we visited Dad's side of the family in Oklahoma, and Grandma kept calling me Sarah and her three fat wiener dogs barked all night, and I hoped we'd never go again. "Not really. It's just me and my mom and dad, so I don't think it'd be any fun. I wish I had a sister."

"We're sisters." Blakely smiled.

Allie nodded. "Yeah."

Warmth filled my chest. I played with the bracelet on my wrist, twirling the charms with our initials. The three of us were chosen sisters, not biological, and that made it even more meaningful.

Allie watched me for a moment, then her eyes flashed with a mischievous glint and she looked to Blakely. "Why did Emily get kicked out of school?"

I grinned. I loved this game.

Blakely picked apart a napkin. "Because she stole the principal's money. And then . . ." Blakely looked to me to answer.

The game was called "And Then What" and going third was

hardest because this was the part of the game that decided the trajectory of the story, if it would be boring and flat or wild and entertaining.

"And then what?" Allie repeated to me.

"She used the money to buy supplies to go live in a forest." There was a moment of silence, and I worried it was too simple, too repetitive of our day.

But Allie smirked and looked pleased enough. "Where she found herself living with . . . hermits. Hairy hermits."

Blakely giggled. "But one of the hermits . . . was actually really hot!"

Allie snort-laughed. "And then . . . ?"

Blakely and Allie watched me, eager for my response.

"And then it turned out that the hot hermit was actually Ryan Gosling's long-lost bastard son," I said, not even knowing where the words came from, just that memories of *The Notebook* were flashing through my mind, and it felt right.

Allie gasped, pressing her hands to her cheeks.

"Oh my goooood." Blakely cackled.

The game continued. Normally, we ran out of interesting ways to keep making the story funnier by turn seven, but this story kept going, evolving into a tale of inbred Ryan Gosling hermits who lived in an expansive cave system beneath the forest and eventually found a portal to an alternate dimension where normal people lived in caves and hermits were the ones who lived in houses.

The three of us doubled over, laughing so hard, chocolate milk came out of our noses. Ruth came over and told us to shut up or else we'd be looking at strike two.

◎

After dinner, we walked as a group with the rest of the campers back to our cabins. The other campers dispersed to theirs while Blakely, Allie, and I had to continue on for another few hundred feet to cabin ten. A couple lamps illuminated our way, but they were old and flickering and covered with so many bugs that the light was practically eclipsed. We were still giggling from our game at dinner, but now, the exhaustion from the day's adventure in the woods was starting to hit me.

My calves and feet ached. The blisters on my heels had popped, and now there was open skin chafing against my shoes. I wanted to pass out right away, but I really needed to cleanse my wounded heels and wash my body of all its salt, sweat, and dirt. My teeth felt fuzzy. No matter how tired I was, I couldn't fathom ever going to bed without a shower and brushing my teeth. Sometimes Blakely went to bed without brushing her teeth and it disgusted me. Millions of bacteria lived in our mouths, eating away at our gums, and if given enough time, they would eat all the way through your gums and up through your brain. I'd told her that before and she still didn't care.

At last, we reached our cabin; I went inside to grab the bathroom supplies I kept beneath my bed. I was already dreading having to walk back down the hill to the showers, but the sooner I got it over with, the better. I pulled out everything I needed from my suitcase and paused. There was a strange sound, a faint buzzing in the air, the fluttering of insect wings. What the hell was that?

I checked behind me. Allie and Blakely stood there, watching me. Allie clasped her hands to her mouth, laughing, while Blakely looked sick. What had they done? I flipped on the lights.

A cloud of gnats hovered above my pillow and a trail of ants crawled from the pillow to under the blanket and down my bed. The spaghetti and chocolate milk churned in my stomach.

"What did you do?" I asked, my voice cracking. I reached to pull the blanket back, hesitating. What horrible thing would I find under there? *What if there's a hair-doll filled with bloody teeth?* What if this wasn't Allie's doing at all but, instead, I'd awoken something terrible in the woods when I'd disturbed the hair-doll and now a tooth demon was here to punish me?

"Ready for bed, Bina?" Allie asked, giggling. "We put a treat on your mattress."

I turned to see the smug grin on her stupid face—the same grin she wore when she signed me up for camp and pushed me into the lake and let me walk around school with a sign taped to my back that said Fat Lezzo Loser—and I knew that whatever happened to my bed had nothing to do with the woods people.

The only threat in my life was right here in this room with me.

Chapter 19

2023

A loud knock on the bedroom door startles me from a deep sleep.

"It's time to party!" Lucas shouts. "Get up, babe!"

I blink awake, rubbing the gunk from my eyes. Party? I glance at my phone. It's 8:00 p.m. I slept the whole afternoon. I push myself upright, my mind groggy, limbs heavy, the wound on my palm burning. It better be healed by Tuesday morning because I am not wasting a moment getting back into the gym and my safe, predictable routine.

I brush my teeth and put on fresh sweatpants, then go to the living room, where Eli, Lucas, and Heather are sitting cross-legged on the hardwood floor, the lights dimmed. A Doors song plays from a Bluetooth speaker, Jim Morrison's deep vocals thrumming over a keyboard chorus. This looks like we're about to do drugs.

"DMT," Eli says, holding up a vape cartridge. "Also known as the Spirit Molecule."

Yep, drugs.

"It's a hallucinogenic that unlocks the wildest parts of your brain. But to really see the good stuff, you need experience with it," Eli continues. "So, don't worry if your first trip is underwhelming."

I sit on the floor between Heather and Lucas. I've heard of DMT before on a podcast that Lucas listened to, and I'm not sure I want to try it at all. If the rumors about DMT "opening your mind" are true, then I should run away. I don't need my mind opened any more. I need it closed.

"This stuff is life-changing," Eli continues, cupping the cartridge like it's a god-blessed chalice. "It opens you up to a whole new world. Peels back the walls of reality and lets you see what's really, really there, takes you to other realms and dimensions. Even out here in the woods, the green looks duller compared to when I'm on a DMT trip. Once my neck—and Heather will confirm this is really true—it was all stiff, locked up after I wiped out snowboarding. I kept heating it, massaging it. Nothing would help. I took a hit of DMT, and I felt these hands on my neck. Warm, strong hands." Eli mimes how these DMT hands massaged his neck. "They came from another realm and put my neck back into place, released all my pain because they could see what I couldn't. When I came to, my neck felt the best it ever had."

Heather nods in agreement. "It's true."

I resist the urge to scoff. I'm pretty sure the DMT made Eli's muscles relax, which was what cured his pain, not DMT-god hands. But I keep that to myself since I don't want to be a party pooper. "You two better never make that statement public," I say. "You could run physical therapy out of business."

Lucas laughs.

"Like I said"—Eli hands the vape to Lucas—"you might not see much on your first trip. Take a good inhale. Then just close your eyes and let it happen."

Lucas puts the cartridge to his lips and inhales, his eyelids fluttering. "Hmm. Tastes like corn chips." He leans back onto the floor, hands folded behind his head. "Whoa."

"What do you see—" I start.

Eli shushes me. "Don't interrupt."

I roll my eyes, but part of me gets it. We all have to believe in something to keep us going. For Eli and Heather, it's this hippie spirituality, souls and stuff—Heather thinks *chickens* have souls—while for me, it's the barbell and Lucas. To each their own.

We sit there, watching Lucas lie on his back with his eyes closed, smiling. A couple minutes later, Lucas sits up, alert and normal looking, without any of the sluggishness I had expected. "That was . . . interesting," he says.

"Are you still high?" I ask. "Do I look different?" I wave my hand in front of his face.

He takes my hand, kissing it. "No. I feel totally fine now."

"One of the best parts of DMT," Eli says, "is that the high only lasts a few minutes. There's no hangover, no lasting high. I take a hit in the mornings before my meetings."

Heather playfully slaps his arm.

I should be alarmed that Eli starts his mornings with psychedelics, but maybe that is normal crypto-bro culture.

"So, what did you see?" Eli asks Lucas.

"A tunnel full of color." Lucas gestures with his hands. "And I was blasting through it, stars and rainbows washing over me. I could *smell* the colors. I could smell purple."

I'm pretty sure he's describing the Rainbow Road level of Mario Kart, but I nod along and say, "Wow, cool."

"Not bad for a first timer," Eli says. "We'll each go one at a time, so we can keep an eye on each other, make sure no one runs away and jumps into the river or something."

I give Heather a worried look.

"He's exaggerating," she reassures me.

I wish I had my phone. If I could, I would be googling "what's the worst that can happen on DMT," hoping I would find something to prove that I shouldn't take it, something that would give me an out. I'm aware that I could, in theory, just say no, but how would Lucas react to that?

Heather takes a hit from the cartridge. She leans back, giggling with her eyes closed. A few minutes later, she sits up. "Oh my god. It was so beautiful." She wipes a tear from her cheek. "I was in the forest. You, Lucas, Eli—you were all there, except, we were kids." Her eyes shine. "All the leaves on the trees had faces, and they danced with us—" Her voice cracks, and she hands the cartridge to me. "You have to try it, Sade."

The cartridge is heavier than I expected. *No thanks*, lingers in the back of my throat, trapped and squirming like a dying mouse caught on a glue trap. But Normal Sadie would not say no, would she?

"Don't worry." Heather squeezes my shoulder. "Like Eli said, the high really is short and you probably won't see much."

"The first time is very underwhelming," Eli adds. "I promise."

Even if it is a bad trip, a few minutes should be fine. Once, I suffered through a layover at LAX on a fifty-milligram edible. (I didn't realize I was only supposed to eat a quarter of the brownie, not the whole thing.) It was a three-hour, nauseating high that had me holding on to an airport bench for dear life, muttering to myself "you can't overdose on weed, you can't overdose on weed."

If I made it through that, I can handle a little DMT. Besides, I'm used to seeing horrible visions by breakfast. I hold the cartridge to my lips and inhale. The taste is salty and, yes, reminiscent of corn chips. I lie back, my hands at my sides on the hardwood floor.

At first, there's nothing special. Just a spinning, falling sensation, the same kind I get when I'm trying to fall asleep on a sleeping pill. I look to my side and gasp.

I'm not falling—I'm *flying*.

Wings have sprouted from my back, great fleshy, muscular ones made of human skin, and I'm spinning because I'm not using them. I need to fix that. I spread my arms and flex my wings—they shoot out from under me like a bat's, my fingertips and red-painted nails at the edges. I soar upward into the night sky, my stomach lurching from the velocity. I fly through clouds, their misty texture cool and soft on my skin. Dew clings to my clothing and hair, making me glisten.

Above me is the moon. It's a giant, veiny, white eyeball marred by a deep vertical crater, and I realize it's not a crater, but a pupil. The eyeball swivels to watch me as I glide beneath it. Below me is the earth, dark and still except for a glow of firelight in the distance.

There's a feeling deep in my belly, an urge, like hunger or thirst, that tells me I'm supposed to go there. *Go to the light.*

I fly toward this mysterious light. It's coming from the bottom of a cave, deep in the ground. I tuck my wings in at my sides and plunge downward headfirst, like a bird diving for fish.

Down.

Down.

Down I go until I enter the earth.

Here in the cave, the air is warmer, humid. I flap my wings to slow myself, hovering until my feet touch soil. A man sits beside a small fire pit on the ground. He is a shadow. Featureless. A silhouette sitting with his elbow rested on his knee. The sight of him should be scary, but I'm not afraid. Instead, I feel relief, like I've finally come home.

The shadow stands. My wings retract into my back. The shadow and I take a step toward each other. He takes my hands. His touch is cold, but the feeling sends waves of warmth through my body.

Sabrina, the voice says, and of course, I know this voice. I knew it would be him. *How are you?*

Something sad and longing twists in my chest, and I realize it's because this simple question is one Lucas never asks me. "Good."

You can tell me the truth.

I sigh. That's what I love so much about Damon: I can be honest with him. "I'm tired. I'm annoyed."

Of?

"Of this trip. Pretending to enjoy it. Of Lucas." I wince for saying it. "Not our relationship, I mean. I just wish he was different sometimes."

Different how?

"Not such an asshole." I laugh at my honesty. "Not so loud. Not so selfish."

We sit in silence. I rest my head against his chest. I don't expect to hear anything, but there is a heartbeat. A soothing, slow *thump, thump, thump.*

What do you want? Damon asks, another question Lucas, or anyone, never asks me.

"Like, in life?"

Yes.

I think for a moment, my fingers interlaced with Damon's invisible ones. "To be happy, I guess?"

You can be. Damon squeezes my hand. *There's just one thing you have to do.*

"What is it?" I ask, feeling as though I'll do whatever it is, whatever Damon wants.

The shadow puts his fingers under my chin, tilting my head up so I'm looking at his face. Even though he has no eyes, I can feel the tension of his powerful gaze holding mine.

You have to kill him, Damon says.

"Who?" I ask, though I fear I already know the answer.

You have to kill Lucas.

Chapter 20

2006

I whipped the blanket back and gagged. A swarm of ants trailed up and down the mattress. There were more gnats, too, but several were trapped in a sticky substance. It smelled sweet. Like maple pancakes, and I understood: The girls had poured syrup all over my bed.

"Oh crap," Blakely said. "We didn't think that would happen."

"No." Allie giggled. "But this is even better."

I quickly wiped the tears forming in my eyes and turned around to face them. "*What* did you mean to happen exactly?"

"We thought we'd put syrup on the bed and then you'd lay down and get all sticky." Blakely groaned. "It was supposed to be funny."

My mouth hung open, my fingers and toes curling with rage.

I slung my bath bag around my shoulder. I couldn't believe it. My friends weren't just bitches—they were stupid bitches.

"I guess you have to snuggle up with the bugs tonight," Allie said. "Aren't they your favorite?"

I ignored her, wondering where the hell I was going to sleep.

"You can fit on my bed with me," Blakely offered.

I shook my head. I knew she wasn't the instigator and was only Allie's henchman. Still, I was just as mad at her. There was no way I was sharing her bed.

"We'll change the sheets, then," Blakely said. "There's spares in the dresser."

"Whatever." I turned to leave. I just needed to shower, then I could come back and deal with this mess.

"Don't be such a brat," Allie said. "It's a prank. Learn to laugh for once, Bina."

I stopped in the doorway. "My name is *Sabrina*!" I shouted, but my voice cracked and it didn't sound as tough as I wanted. I fumbled with the clasp around my wrist, got my friendship bracelet off, and threw it at the wall. It clinked and fell to the floor.

Allie was a liar—we weren't sisters.

Sisters didn't torture each other like this.

And for once in my life, I was angry enough to say what I really thought, so I yelled, "And you're a stupid mean bitch!"

Allie's face fell. Her eyes darkened. Redness crept up her neck, and her hair seemed to rise with anger. She looked like a witch about to curse me.

My stomach tightened and I immediately regretted what I'd said. I hurried outside, slamming the door behind me. I glanced over my shoulder to make sure Allie and Blakely weren't following, and I noticed something taped to the door. A folded piece of notebook paper. I hadn't seen it when we came back to the cabin, so either I hadn't been paying close enough attention or someone had just put it up. I doubled back to grab the note and walked toward the showers, unfolding the paper.

In the center were three stick-figure girls crudely drawn with colored pencils. The one on the left had long straight blonde hair. The one in the center had wavy auburn hair. And the one on the right had dark frizzy hair and a round belly. I supposed that one was supposed to be me. *What the hell, Allie?* She must've put this note up when we got back to the cabin. More anger ignited in me.

I walked under a lamp to get a closer look. The stick-figure girls had spirals for eyes, which made us look hypnotized. Or dead. Allie's stick figure was smiling, while mine and Blakely's had straight lines for mouths, like we felt nothing.

"Okaaay," I said aloud and sarcastically, stuffing the piece of paper in my pocket. Obviously, Allie was trying to scare me. They were always doing this kind of crap: locking me in the closet and telling me there's a ghost behind me, emailing me YouTube videos that start out with a puppy playing and then suddenly there's a jump-scare demon on the screen. *Filling my bed with bugs!*

Being here at camp must've made them have to think outside the box. But wasn't putting syrup in my bed enough of a prank? Why would they do the creepy drawing prank *and* the bed prank back-to-back? Even I knew that there had to be some time between these things or else it was just overkill and not funny.

I stopped in the middle of the trail and took the note out

again, my stomach slowly sinking. *What if this isn't from Allie and Blakely?*

What if this isn't just a dumb prank, but a real threat?

But from who? The Gríma Wormtongue woman?

I turned to look back at our cabin. Should I go back and tell Allie and Blakely?

No.

For the first time in my life, I'd just stood up for myself. I couldn't go crawling back now. I put the note in my pocket. Even if I showed it to Allie and Blakely, they would probably make fun of me and say that I was making a big thing out of nothing.

But then again, maybe this note was just what I needed to convince them that the evil things I'd told them about in the woods—they were all true.

Chapter 21

2023

Before anyone else is awake, I sit on the couch, lacing up my running shoes. I haven't gone on a run in the three years since I started lifting. There's no need to: The energy system used for running is counterproductive to the energy system used for lifting, the endorphin release piddling compared to the rush of lifting heavy weights. I'm sure this run will suck, but I need to do something physical.

I need to push my body.

I need to sweat.

I need to distract myself from that DMT trip last night and get Damon's words out of my head. I can still hear him now.

You have to kill Lucas.

The Mean Ones

It's just an intrusive thought, I tell myself in my ex-therapist's voice. *Damon's not real. The DMT made you think your deepest, most unthinkable, thoughts.*

But I've never had intrusive thoughts like this before.

I have the common ones: What if I jump over this cave ledge? What if I drive headfirst into oncoming traffic? What if I stick my fingers in between the metal plates of the pulldown machine? Never has the thought of hurting—let alone killing—Lucas ever crossed my mind. Never has an intrusive thought felt so pervasive, so . . . I cringe thinking the word: *appealing*.

I jump up from the couch, shaking out my arms and legs, like if I just move enough, I can shake the bad thoughts out of my brain and body. A cough comes from Heather and Eli's bedroom down the hall. I leave through the back door, shutting it quietly behind me. I don't want to bump into Heather and Eli: In fact, I'm going to avoid them as much as possible today. Last night, when I came back to reality after my DMT trip, Eli and Heather tried to pry out every detail about what I saw. I lied, telling them vague things about colors and tunnels, parroting what Lucas had said.

My DMT trip wasn't supposed to be so vivid, so real. They said it wouldn't be like that, and part of me feels betrayed, like they sent me to a dark otherworldly place I wasn't supposed to go.

But then again, they don't know that my mind already sees things that it shouldn't.

Once I'm a safe couple hundred meters from the cabin, I bend down, stretching my hamstrings. It's a brisk morning, the sun hidden behind the clouds, the river's gentle current glistening. I head down the gravel path at a slow jog, my breath quickening. I take the first trail off the river toward the road. Running along the roadside feels safer than going into the forest, and I won't go far. I'll stay within a few hundred meters of the cabin, passing it back and forth until my body is good and tired. I head down the hill, the strength of my legs making my strides feel powerful, surprisingly easy.

A quarter mile in, I'm jogging so well, I figure I can just run laps by the cabin all morning. I can return when the others have forgotten all about the DMT and won't ask me about it again. But what if they want to do it again tonight? I groan. Maybe I can fall asleep early or feign illness. *You could just say no.* The thought spikes my anxiety; avoiding the problem is so much easier.

I speed up my jogging pace into a run, trying not to think about anything but the strides of my legs and the pleasurable burn in my lungs. And while my legs are pumping beneath me, those bad thoughts do diminish. A minute later, a stitch forms on my side, a stabbing ache between my ribs. My calves tighten, stiff as metal cords. My stamina comes to a hard stop. I slow to a limping half walk, half jog, sucking in air. These legs are definitely made for squatting, not running.

I'm coming up on the large boulder I've passed a few times. I hobble toward it and sit on the rock, taking in slow, deep breaths. Tension spreads across my forehead, the warning signs of a blinding headache. I definitely did not drink enough water for this type of exertion. I close my eyes.

The piney scent of the woods takes me back to my days at

The Mean Ones

Camp Graywood, to the day I spent lost in the forest. I can see it all like it just happened yesterday: the ancient spiral tree, the hair-doll, the demon deer. I know what will happen if I keep thinking these thoughts, so I try my usual defense mechanism of planning my exercise routine. *Once I get home, I'm going to start a new Smolov Squat cycle—I'll do two-a-day training sessions, an early morning strength session and an evening bodybuilding session.*

The plans to return to normal soothe the bad thoughts, the images of the hair-doll and demon deer melting away, replaced by visions of me squatting double my body weight. It's all good now. I open my eyes. My stomach buckles, my heart knocking in my chest. I blink a few times, startled by the vividness of the Other Place.

The sky is red, casting a crimson hue over the forest. The trees are upside down, leaves growing into the ground, gnarled roots curling upward toward the blood-red sky. Worms and beetles fall from the roots, plopping to the ground, where they wriggle and thrash, disoriented. Dirt drifts down from the roots like brown snow.

White tendrils glide through the air, ghostly and translucent, swirling about like limbs of a jellyfish. I reach out to touch one and feel nothing. Of course I don't feel anything, because none of this is real. It can't be. This is just my mind, my imaginary world.

Still, I can't help but look around the inverted forest in awe. Aside from that time in the cave, the Other Place has never looked so fantastical before, has never felt so much like I've entered a whole new realm. A jolt of panic hits me: What if I'm still high from the DMT?

No.

No way.

Eli said it only lasts a few minutes. But how do I know what time feels like on DMT? *What if I'm still in the DMT world? What if I'm trapped there and can't get out?*

My limbs tingle with anxiety. I pinch myself and it hurts as much as I expected to; I don't know what it proves, but it seemed like something I should do.

I turn around to head back for the cabin, but the road I'd run down now curves sharply to the right, straight into the forest. I stand on my toes, searching for a clear path back to the cabin, but there is none.

There is no way back to the cabin without entering the woods.

I squeeze my eyes shut. *It's okay.* I start counting: *ten, nine, eight—*

Look, Damon says. *Really look, Sabrina.*

I shake my head. I don't want to look. *Don't call me Sabrina.* I just want to be Normal Sadie. I want to go on a normal jog in the normal world with upright trees and all its normal boring colors. *Please.*

What's so good about being normal? he asks.

I stammer for an answer. I know I have a good reason but can't put it into words right now.

Come to me, Damon says. *I'm right here.*

Invisible fingers lace with mine, ripples of warm current rushing through my veins. I open my eyes, turning to look for Damon. Even though I want to be normal, I also want to know what Damon looks like. I want to know that he is real and not just an imaginary BFF I've held on to for too long. No one is next to me, but I *feel* him, right there.

This way. The invisible hand tugs me toward the trees. *It's okay. You're safe.*

The hand leaves mine, and straight ahead, on the trunk of an upside-down tree, a humanoid shadow manifests, the silhouette tall and lanky. The shadow starts walking, taking long, graceful strides. It drifts across the trees, heading into the forest.

"Damon?" I ask, feeling like a lost lunatic talking to shadows in the woods. Because that's what I've become, isn't it? A crazy woods lady.

The tendrils in the air turn and follow the shadow, floating with it into the trees. I should go back to the cabin, but I want to know if this shadow is really Damon and where he is going. I want to feel that warm rushing sensation I only get when he touches me.

I consider my options: I can sit on this rock, waiting for the world to turn normal or for someone to save me. Or I can follow the shadow. But what if there's danger in the forest? *I'm an adult now*, I remind myself. A strong, beefy adult. I may not have much running stamina, but I can sure as hell sprint and fight. *Plus, Damon's here.* I catch up to the shadow, running on the road until it disintegrates into a dirt path. I follow the shadow deeper into the forest, the upside-down trees growing denser, the red sun peeking through the roots overhead.

When the shadow crosses a narrow stream and a knotted fallen log, I recognize this path as the one that leads to the cave. We still have a ways to go, but I'm sure we're headed there. I stop and lean against a tree, looking back to see if the road is still visible.

Something moves on the bark beneath my hand. I jerk back. The bumps and lines on the trunk are slithering up and down, curving like smiles. A few spots in the lines open and close, exposing gaping, fleshy holes with moist mucous membranes. A human groan comes from one of the holes, and then another cries out. I turn to the other trees—they're embedded with dozens of mouths, gums riddled with little craters where teeth should be. One lets out a blood-curdling scream. Another laughs. Then the trunks of all the trees around me begin to ripple, hundreds of mouths screaming and crying and laughing, their noise deafening.

I cover my ears, turning back to the path. I quicken my pace, trying not to look at the trees, trying not to listen to the voices. Some are high-pitched and girlish while others are deep and masculine.

Sabrina's here.

Our Sabrina.

Come home.

Come here.

Come back.

My blood turns cold. My hands go numb, my breaths shallow, a panic attack threatening to overtake me. The humanoid shadow doubles back.

Breathe, Damon says. *You're okay.*

I shake my head.

I won't let anything bad happen to you.

Part of me knows that's true, but I don't trust myself to discern what's real and what's not. I come to an abrupt stop. I'm not alone anymore: There's a woman standing ahead on the trail, her back to me. She's pale-skinned and barefoot, wearing a dirty white dress. Something is tied around the back of her head. A mask. Antlers stick up out of her messy hair.

"Hello?" I say.

Without answering, she darts into the woods.

I approach where she'd been standing. On the ground is a folded paper, pinned in place by a small rock. I bend down and open the note. It's a crude drawing of four people, their eyes tightly wound spirals. A woman with long blonde hair, a man with muscular shoulders, another man with a beard and dark hair pulled up in a bun, and a woman with dark hair and big shoulders. My hands shake, the familiarity of the drawing making my blood pressure spike.

Beneath the drawing are the words: *Leave or Die.*

I crumple the note and throw it on the ground. *It's not real.* This is the Other Place. Soon it will pass and the note and Damon's voice and the upside-down trees and the weird tendrils in the air will all be gone. *Toes, ankles, knees*, I repeat, flexing my muscles. *I'm going to open my eyes and everything will be normal.*

Something cold and sharp grabs my arm. I shriek, whipping around to see a creature staring back at me. Its toothless mouth hangs open. Blood stains its leathery nostrils. Dark brown human eyes glare at me from behind the deer's crusty eyeholes.

"Take your friends and go," the woman in the mask says. She's still gripping my arm, her sharp nails digging into my skin. Her hands are stained a drying rust-colored red. She must be the woman I saw the night before at the river. Is she real or part of my hallucinations?

"Why are you following me?" I yank my arm back.

"To make sure you leave this place."

"Why?" Tears prickle my eyes.

"Just go, now."

Her mask looks just like the deer mask the woman wore at Camp Graywood. And her height, her sunspotted skin—she *looks* just like the woman from Camp Graywood. The recognition is almost comforting: She can't be real if this is the same woman who killed my friends. This whole thing is another PTSD nightmare, just my memory reliving the trauma.

"*Hurry.* The cabin is that way." She points behind me. "Get in your car and go."

Damon's shadow hovers on the tree line. *Don't listen to her*, he says. He stops, waiting for me.

Something deep in my chest tugs at me to go toward him, but the sensible part of me knows it would be better to go back to the cabin, to choose normal over whatever this is.

I turn around and run.

Chapter 22

2006

I speed-walked to the showers, paranoid that something was out there in the woods, watching me. The inky gray clouds parted to expose a full moon, yellow and enormous in the night sky. An owl hooted from a tree. Something flew by, wings flapping aggressively. I upped my pace to a half jog, the darkness tightening all around, like a cold, unwanted hug.

The note in my back pocket felt hot, alive, like it was wriggling against my skin. Part of me wanted to throw it on the ground and leave it behind, but another part of me knew it was important, that I had to show it to Allie and Blakely. Even though I was pissed and never wanted to talk to them again, I couldn't keep this to myself. If it turned out that Allie had made the note, then she'd laugh and call me stupid and so what—I'd been through all of that before. But if it wasn't Allie's drawing, if it really was from some weirdo in the woods, then I needed my friends on my side. The thought of sharing the note with Allie and Blakely was almost exciting—we could solve a camp mystery.

In a brief final sprint, I made it into the shower building where the fluorescent lights provided safety from the outside darkness and all its flying, flapping creatures. I took the note from my pants and put it in a pocket of my bag, then I undressed and stepped into the shower, wetting my hair and shampooing it before the hot water petered out to lukewarm. The water rinsed away the grime on my skin and loosened my aching muscles. I ran a pink BIC razor across my armpits. I couldn't help but notice the dark hairs on my forearms; when wet, they looked even longer and darker.

Tomorrow, we were going to the lake again. I cringed remembering how last time Allie had made fun of my hairy arms. I held the razor above my forearm. If I shaved them, then they would be smooth like Allie's, and wouldn't Jesse prefer a girl without hairy arms? He would, I was sure, and that's all I needed to make my decision. I ran the razor down my arm, the black hairs clogging up the blades. I rinsed the hair away and decided it'd be better to go against the hair to get a closer shave. A few minutes later, I had two hairless, buttery-smooth arms. For once, I felt beautiful, glossy and pristine, like Arwen in *The Fellowship of the Ring*.

The moment I dried myself off, my arms broke out in furious itching. I rubbed lotion on them, only for the itching to evolve into burning itching. Angry red bumps erupted over my skin. My stomach rolled with regret. What had I done? Only one thing could be worse than hairy arms: rashy arms.

It's okay, I told myself while changing into my pajamas. Surely, my skin would calm down by morning. It had to or else I'd have to come up with a way to get out of going to the lake tomorrow. I stood at the sink, brushing my teeth.

The main door on the other side of the lockers swung open. Another girl must've been coming in to shower. I finished brushing my teeth and put on my pajama pants. Allie and Blakely didn't seem to mind being seen naked by other girls, but I hated it. I supposed that if I had a conventionally skinny, girlish body then I wouldn't mind either, but I did not, and now with my red, bumpy arms I felt more like the cave troll from the mines of Moria than Arwen or any girl Jesse would ever like. The thought made me want to cry.

I had a sweatshirt in my bag, and I put it on even though it was hot and stuffy. There was no way I was going to let Allie or anyone else see my rashy arms. It was going to be uncomfortably hot trying to sleep tonight, and then I remembered with a choking half cry, half laugh that I didn't even have a bed to sleep in because mine was infested with bugs.

I spritzed leave-in conditioner into my hair, waiting for whoever had entered the building to round the corner, but she didn't. Instead, I heard heavy, raspy breathing. The aggravated breathing of an angry, big, hooved animal; wet snorting through bovine nostrils.

I set my brush down, the hairs on the back of my neck rising. "Hello?"

I hoped it was just a big, heavy-breathing girl. Maybe she was sick and congested. But the breathing felt too inhuman . . . too reminiscent of the creature in the woods. The breathing quickened, followed by a snarl. My heart throbbed in my neck.

I packed up my bag, my shaking hands knocking my hairbrush and conditioner to the floor. I bent down to grab them, purposefully not looking up or in the mirror. I slung my bag around my shoulder and crouch-ran for the door, not checking behind me. If I didn't look back, if I didn't see the monster, then it wasn't real.

I ran outside, and only when I was a few yards from the shower building did I look back. Other kids were walking into the showers, chatting like nothing was amiss. I sighed. Nothing had followed me. It was okay. I was safe. I was probably imagining that same breathing I'd heard from the demon deer earlier. The creepy note had me overreacting.

I turned toward my cabin and started walking. A quarter of the way there, I saw Jesse Pierce. He was across the dirt path with his hands in his pockets, slowly pacing back and forth. His sideswept light brown hair hung gently around his left cheek. Beneath the glow of lamplight and the full moon, he looked as beautiful as ever. Angelic.

Why is he out here? But did it really matter why? The fact was that Jesse Pierce was here and alone, and I was clean—my hair conditioned, my teeth brushed, my pits freshly shaved and deodorized. Rashy arms aside, this was the best I was ever going to smell and look. Maybe the universe had decided I was finally due for something positive, and so it had planted Jesse right there in front of me.

The Mean Ones

I took a step forward. What was I going to say? What if I showed him the creepy note? I took it out from my bag and smoothed out the wrinkles. It would be a good icebreaker. Memorable. Instead of Allie and Blakely, Jesse and I could solve the camp mystery together. We could spend the night searching for clues and throw a net over the bad guy. We would be like Arwen and Aragorn, defeating the evil in the woods. My heart swelled with tingling joy. A grin spread across my face.

I took another step forward, about to call out Jesse's name, when Allie skipped down the path. Jesse's face lit up at the sight of her. She twirled her hair around her finger the way she did around a boy she liked. Allie's hand went for Jesse's, and he took it, her dainty pink-nailed hand in his.

My stomach twisted with sharp pain, like several magnets were winding through my guts, piercing my membranes and killing me slowly.

My Jesse was holding Allie's hand.

Two days ago, Allie hadn't even known Jesse's name.

Allie and Jesse stepped closer to the trees, hiding in case an adult walked by, but I could see everything. The magnets in my guts kept tearing through me, ripping through my stomach lining all the way up to my heart. Tears clouded my vision, but I still saw it: Allie standing on her tippy-toes, kissing Jesse on the lips.

The note fell from my hands. The wind blew it away.

"I'm really sorry," Blakely said once I walked back into our cabin. "I changed out the sheets and wiped it down. Look, no bugs."

I nodded, my mind and body numb. I needed to curl up in a dark place and disappear from the world, like a wounded cat ready to die. I pulled my suitcase out from under the bed.

"What are you doing?" Blakely asked. "You're not leaving, right?"

I shook my head. I threw my pillow and fresh blanket under the bed, then got on my hands and knees and crawled beneath the bed frame, letting the sheet drape over the side so I was concealed. The closed, tight space felt safe, not as comforting as being under my bed back home, but it was better than being out in the room.

"You're sleeping under there?" Blakely asked.

"Yep." I rolled onto my side, praying I could fall asleep before Allie returned. Though maybe she wouldn't come back at all. Maybe she'd spend the night in the woods with Jesse, living out the fantasy I'd had about us. A knot clogged the back of my throat. I pulled my knees to my chest.

"Where's Allie?" Blakely asked.

My eyes narrowed. Blakely's tone was innocent but there was no way she didn't know what Allie had been planning with Jesse. She was probably even her wingman.

"With a boy." Jesse's name was too painful to speak.

"Oh."

She didn't ask which boy, so she probably knew it was Jesse. I closed my eyes, but the angry pounding in my head made it impossible to sleep, the pain in my chest all-encompassing. My body ached and shivered like I had the flu. I tossed and turned and used the pillow to stifle my sobs.

Sometime later, Allie came back into the cabin. It felt like it had been a long time, long enough for Allie and Jesse to have fallen in love and gotten engaged. I curled into a tighter fetal position until I was a near-perfect ball. Conglobation. That's what it's called when pill bugs do this to shield themselves from predators.

"Where's Bina?" Allie asked.

"Under there." Blakely must've been pointing at my bed.

"Oh," Allie replied. "Weird."

"So . . . how was it?" Blakely asked.

I could feel Allie glowing and grinning, joy radiating off her. "Amazing, Jesse is so—" she started to say. I covered my ears, mentally going *lalalalalala*, but I could still hear Allie and Blakely squealing and giggling. I prayed for a meteor to strike the cabin, for an earthquake to erupt and swallow us into the earth, for that demon deer to show up and shred us to bits. I prayed for something—anything—to kill us all. Eventually, I fell asleep to the images of us all dying violent deaths.

I stirred awake to the sound of the door creaking open.

Chapter 23

2023

When I make it back to the river path, the world has reverted to its normal state: The trees are upright again, the sky a gray blue instead of red. I should be relieved that I'm no longer in the Other Place, but I can't help feeling that this regular world is bland. Underwhelming. I get what Eli meant when he said that the real world is duller compared to his DMT world. A deep, primal part of me yearns for the strange, inverted beauty of the Other Place, for Damon, and what if I should listen to that part of me? What if I should stop trying to resist it?

I shake my head. I shouldn't think like that. *Normal Sadie wants the Normal world!*

I stagger back up to the cabin, clutching my aching side. I haven't run that fast since middle school PE. In the kitchen, I take the cold jug of water from the fridge, my shaking hands spilling half of it on the counter as I fill a glass. I drink, closing my eyes, focusing on the sensation of the cold water on the back of my throat. *Toes, ankles, knees.* But the masked woman's words and the note keep replaying in my mind: *Leave or die.*

I set the glass down, leaning against the counter, inhaling and exhaling slowly. *She wasn't real*, I repeat.

But she had looked and felt so real while the rest of the Other Place had been so dreamlike. I fill the glass with more water, my chest tightening. Hypothetically, what if she *was* real? Even if I wanted to heed her advice, how could I convince Lucas to leave? I gulp down the water, considering my options. If I tried to get Lucas to pack up and go because some woman in a deer mask in the woods said so, he would blow a fuse. I wouldn't exactly blame him.

I glance at the clock on the microwave. It's only 7 a.m. Lucas will still be sleeping; maybe I can crawl back into bed with him and start the day over again. I walk down the hall to our room, stepping quietly so I don't wake anyone, but when I pass Heather and Eli's room, their hushed voices carry through the door. I'm not one to eavesdrop on my friends, but I hear Eli say my name. I stop, curiosity getting the better of me.

"Well, *when* are we going to tell Sadie?" Eli says impatiently.

"She's not ready," Heather says.

I'm not ready for what? Random scenarios flash through my mind: Maybe they got me a present, or they're going to spring something terrible on me like a skydiving trip.

"When will she be ready?" Eli presses. "We can't keep waiting.

It's been long enough."

It's probably something about them. Maybe Heather's pregnant. The thought makes me a little sad, like she's catapulting forward through all the big life stages while I'm still stuck in the past and stagnant in the present.

There are more muffled words, Eli's tone escalating from impatience to irritation.

"If Willow doesn't quit her antics, we're going to have a problem," Heather snaps. "Her jealousy could screw this whole thing up."

I should leave now—the conversation has moved past me, but I'm curious. *Who is Willow and what is getting screwed up?*

Eli says something indiscernible but cranky.

Heather responds: "We have to. For my sister."

Heather has a sister? Jehovah's Witnesses are all about pro-birth, so she might have a dozen sisters for all I know, but she's never mentioned any sisters before, and I'm a little hurt that I didn't know that important detail about my best friend. The floor creaks like one of them is getting up; I hurry down the hall to the bathroom.

After rinsing the sweat from my body, I crawl into bed with Lucas, relishing the warm safety beneath the comforter. Maybe a couple more hours of sleep is all I need to clear my mind and calm down. I close my eyes, rolling over to spoon Lucas. His body is toasty, soothing, and my mind begins to fog over, sleep pulling me into its depths.

There's a rapid *tap, tap, tap* at the window. I pull an extra pillow over my head to dull the noise.

Tap, tap, tap.

I peek through one eye. It must be a branch blowing against the window, scraping the glass. The sound grows more aggressive. Maybe it's a woodpecker.

Tap, tap, tap.

I throw the pillow and blanket off and get up to investigate the tapping. At the window, I whip the curtains back. I stifle a scream.

A dead deer stares back at me—the woman in the mask.

She's holding the note to the window, pointing at the stick-figure drawing of us. Her dark brown eyes bulge behind the deer's dried eyelids.

With a dirty, bony finger, the woman gestures to the words: *Leave or Die.*

I glance around for signs that I'm imagining her again, but there are none. My stomach lurches, bile searing my throat. This is the real world.

The note is real.

The woman is real.

Chapter 24

2006

The sound of the cabin door opening and closing blended into a scene in my dream: I was wandering the aisles of a pet store for fantastical creatures, browsing the pixies and goblins for sale, when another customer entered the store, the door shutting loudly behind them. The customer brought their service unicorn with them, and the glowing white creature took loud steps toward me, whinnying and snorting. The vibration of a foot near my head snapped me awake.

My eyes focused on the metal frame a few inches from my face. I blinked, the comfort of my dream fizzling away. It had been such a good dream; why did it have to be interrupted? The sickening heartbreak of the previous night came back to me like a wet, cold towel being draped over my body. I wiped away the fresh tears forming in my eyes.

The feet beside me took a couple more steps. I glanced to the side, and through the crack between the sheet and floor, I saw a pair of brown boots. *Who is in our cabin?* The boots were adult sized. *Is it Ruth? No.* The calves the boots were connected to looked too thin to be Ruth's. Maybe it was another counselor. *Ugh.* They probably saw the bug-ridden sheets that Blakely put outside and now we were all in trouble. At least I could tell them it was Allie's fault. Maybe I could even tell on her for kissing Jesse and she would get sent home.

"Where is the third girl?" a woman asked, voice low and husky, uncomfortably familiar.

A chill spread across my skin.

Was it the same voice of the woman I'd met in the forest? Why would she be in here?

I waited for Allie or Blakely to point out that I was under my bed, but they were quiet. How could they be sleeping through this? There's no way Blakely was—she was a notoriously light sleeper. I scooted an inch to the side so I could get a better view of the room, peeking out from under the sheet. My stomach buckled. Panic jolted through me. I covered my mouth, scooting deeper under the bed.

There were three adults in the room: two masked women and one man with his back to me, a sack over his head. The shortest one was the Gríma Wormtongue woman I'd seen in the woods earlier. I recognized her pale, waxy skin and the long black hair draping down her back. She was wearing a brown-and-gray rabbit mask now, which looked far too real to have been purchased in any costume store. The fur was dense, double-layered with thick bushy hairs on top of a soft undercoat, big fluffy ears sticking up out of her head.

The other woman also wore a white dress and was taller with sun-spotted tan skin. She was barefoot and had thick yellow toenails that looked more like the horns of an animal than human nails. Her face was concealed by a deer mask, antlers poking up out of her head, the nose wrinkled and leathery, eye holes spotted with crust, lips gaping and smeared with blood.

"Edith, you can take your mask off now," the yellow-toenail woman said, her voice was high-pitched, girlish. She placed her deer mask on the dresser.

Gríma Wormtongue removed her rabbit mask, then the man took the sack off his head.

"I didn't say you could do that," yellow-toenails chastised him.

He silently put it back on.

"But go ahead," yellow-toenails sighed. "Do well tonight and your punishment will be eased." She held a cloth to Allie's mouth while the man held one to Blakely's.

Wake up, I silently pleaded. *Do something, Allie!* But the girls were motionless, their eyes closed.

"The other girl must've switched cabins," yellow-toenails said, annoyed.

"Damn it," Gríma Wormtongue responded. "Will this still work?"

Yellow-toenails considered. "Didn't the girl say she saw him in the woods today? If that's true and he is roaming our plane, then he is hungry. We better pray it works."

What the hell were they talking about? Why wouldn't Allie and Blakely wake up? My pulse pounded in my temples.

"Pick her up," Gríma Wormtongue ordered the man. He turned around—I saw his face clearly now, and I wished I hadn't. I held back a scream and crept deeper under the bed, shutting my eyes.

The man's lips were sewn together, black thread pulled through red, swollen flesh. I'd only seen him for a second, yet the image was seared into my mind. I pinched my arm, hard, hoping this was all part of a heartbreak-induced fever dream. When I opened my eyes, none of this would really be happening.

I opened them, turning my head to peek at the room.

The man was still there, his lips definitely still sewn shut. I held back a sob.

The man picked up Allie easily, like she was made of feathers instead of flesh and bone, and placed her on the floor in a seated position. He stood so her body leaned against his leg to keep her from falling over. She was so limp and unresponsive, I worried she was dead. But her head lolled to the side, and I could see the slight rise and fall of her chest as she breathed.

The yellow-toenail woman carried Blakely over with a little more effort. Then Gríma Wormtongue crouched and tied Blakely's hands behind her back with rope while the man did the same with Allie. A pungent oniony smell wafted through the room, tangy and slightly metallic. The man took a step back toward my bed and the stench strengthened. The stink was them; these people really must've lived in the woods. I covered my nose.

Gríma Wormtongue stuffed rags into Blakely and Allie's mouths. My stomach backflipped. That meant they expected the girls to wake up: Allie and Blakely were going to know what was happening to them—I didn't know what that was exactly, but it felt like it was going in a very bad direction.

The man and yellow-toenail woman worked together to position Allie and Blakely so they were propped up against each other back-to-back, while Gríma Wormtongue began setting up candles around the room. The candles were skinny and a pale flesh color and looked lumpy and homemade. She placed them along the dresser and the floor, and now she was coming closer to me, taking small, crouched steps.

Gríma Wormtongue kneeled by the bed, the sour smell of her BO assaulting my nostrils. I held my breath, lying perfectly still. She was a foot away. What if she saw me?

She placed a candle a few inches from my head, then another at the end of the bed by my feet, and she moved on. I worried I'd spasm in fear and accidentally kick the candle, but I slowly counted backward from ten, and I managed to remain silent and unmoving. Gríma Wormtongue did another loop around the room, this time lighting the candles with a match. The candles smelled like grease burning in a pan. The room got hotter and the burning fat smell mixed in with the BO, making the whole room smell even worse.

Now that there were several candles around the room, I hoped someone would see the light in the windows. Ruth might come to investigate why we had lights on and end up saving us, but I craned my neck to see that the curtains on the windows were drawn. I blinked my tears away.

Gríma Wormtongue approached the dresser where she'd left a wicker basket. She reached in and pulled out a large knife. It was unlike any knife I'd ever seen: off-white with a knobby handle, the edge sharpened to a fine point. It looked like it was made of bone. *Human bone*, I thought, though I couldn't possibly be sure of that.

She passed the knife to yellow-toenails and said, "It is time for the first offer."

Yellow-toenails nodded, taking the knife. She kneeled. I stayed small and pressed to the floor, as still as possible. Yellow-toenails ran the tip of the knife across Blakely's cheek. The skin split with ease, tiny droplets of blood running down her face.

I could scream, I thought. I could scream so loud it would wake Ruth and she would come running to save us. But could my screams really wake Ruth in time? Her cabin was down the hill. These people could easily kill me before she got here.

"Ralac, we offer you life," yellow-toenails said. She held the knife to the side of Blakely's throat, then stuck it in, and with one swift pull, she yanked it through her flesh. Blood gushed out.

A gasping cry escaped me. I covered my mouth, afraid that the adults had heard me, but the noise I'd made was masked by the sound of Blakely's blood rushing out of her, splattering to the floor in a red wave. A sputtering, gagging sound came from Blakely's open throat as her body tried to breathe.

The spilling went on for another minute. On and on it poured, spreading across the floor. The red puddle crept toward me. Closer. Closer. I tried to scoot back but there was nowhere to go. Blakely's warm blood met my bare toes, seeped into my pajamas.

Finally, the blood fall petered out, and one final wet, ragged choke came from Blakely's neck as her body gasped its last breath of air.

Then it was quiet, except for a soft *drip, drip, drip*, the last of Blakely's blood trickling to the floor like a faucet left untightened.

I kept my hands over my mouth, sobbing silently. I had expected more warning, hadn't expected this to escalate so quickly. Why didn't I do something before Blakely died?

Blakely's body slumped off to the side, taking Allie to the floor with her. Their bodies fell so that Allie was facing me. Allie stirred, her head slowly bobbing up and down. Her eyelids fluttered open. After a few confused blinks, her eyes widened at the sight of all the blood beneath her. She thrashed, her screams muffled by the rag, the silver friendship bracelet on her wrist scraping the wooden floor.

I squirmed from the discomfort of my own uselessness. I wanted to help Allie. But how could I?

"Ralac, we offer you a second life. May her pain compensate for our lack of a third," Gríma Wormtongue said. A shudder rippled through me. I didn't like the sound of that at all.

Allie did a little squirming motion on the ground to get away, but it was futile. There was no escape for her.

But for me? The door wasn't far, just a few feet away. And what if I could go get help for Allie?

The two women and the man clasped hands. The women spoke in a strange language that I couldn't understand. But it sounded like the words I'd heard spoken in the forest: backward, guttural English. Then they hummed a low rhythmic tune. The humming grew louder, and the adults kneeled in the blood on the floor, their eyes closed as they sang their crazy song.

I had a clear shot for the door. If I darted for it, I could slip out before they even noticed me.

Their humming intensified, and soon it sounded as if there were far more than just three people, instead hundreds, humming in unison. The voices vibrated through the floor, like people were singing from beneath the ground. The humming carried across the air, so loud it drowned out Allie's muffled cries.

I have to get out of here, and I could do it. The adults were so consumed by their song—their eyes were closed, the humming so loud, they probably wouldn't even hear me opening the door, and even if they did, I would have a head start.

I inched closer to the edge of the bed, readying myself. I glanced at Allie.

She saw me. Her blonde hair clung to her face with sweat and blood, her blue eyes shining with tears. She held my gaze, silently begging for my help.

I pressed my finger to my lips and gave a reassuring nod, gesturing toward the door. Hope flickered across Allie's face.

I gripped the slick, bloody floor, still vibrating from the cacophony of humming voices. The door was right there. Five feet away. I could do it. I wanted to do it.

Three, two, one, I counted. *Go.*

But my legs did not move. My body would not go.

It was fear, I would decide in the days and months and years after the fact. I would rewrite this scene in my mind, adding details about how my legs were rooted to the ground with terror, my muscles frozen. But the truth was this: I looked at Allie, watched her cry in terror with Blakely's dead body tied up against hers, and thought, *You bitch.*

You pushed me into the lake. You call me fat—I'm not even fat, and so what if I was!? You kissed Jesse Pierce. You never take me seriously. You didn't listen to me about the demon deer or woman in the woods, and now Blakley's dead. Blakely's dead because of you.

I chose not to move.

Instead, I crawled back into the safety of my dark crevice under the bed. Allie screamed and kicked harder than ever. The adults finished their humming and stood. Now that the song had ended, the room was eerily quiet but for Allie's muffled cries and the scraping of her bracelet on the floor.

Gríma Wormtongue picked up the bone knife and kneeled by Allie, who thrashed, shaking her head, tears streaming down her face. Gríma pressed the tip of the knife into Allie's thigh, the flesh caving beneath the blade, and I wanted to look away . . . but a stronger, deeper part of me that I'd never felt before—it wanted to watch.

Chapter 25

2023

I jump back from the window. "Lucas, look!"

He groans and pulls a pillow over his head.

I rush over and yank it off him. "Get up!" This is my chance to show him that I'm not crazy—he has to see that the woman in the deer mask is real.

He scowls at me. "What is your problem?"

"There's a woman at the window!" I yell. "Come look, *now*!" If he sees her and the note, then he'll see the danger for himself. He'll realize we have to go. "Hurry!"

Lucas sits up. He glances toward the window, shielding his eyes from the sun.

I turn and point to where she was. But no one is there now, just the branch of a tree drifting in the wind, leaves scraping the window. Her handprint left a smudge on the glass—proof she was really here. "Look!" I shout, relieved that I have tangible evidence. "That's where she touched the window!"

Lucas squints, then shakes his head. "Come back to bed."

I have no choice. I have to go get her. I run out of the bedroom and down the hall for the back door. I loop around the side of the house, barefoot, rocks and sticks sharp on my feet. When I make it to the rear side of the house, she's not there. I search for her footprints on the ground, but the earth is cluttered with too many ferns and leaves for me to discern anything useful. "Hello?" I call. "Woods lady? Are you still here?"

A bird chirps. The wind rustles the trees. A cicada sings its noisy mating song.

I groan in frustration. Maybe she left the note somewhere. I bend down, searching the bushes, looking for a place she could have stuck it.

"What the hell are you doing!?" Lucas shouts, opening the window. Something lumpy and white falls off the window ledge. I rush forward and pick it up. It's the note, crumpled around a rock. I unfold it and sigh with relief when I see the stick-figure drawing of us and the warning: *Leave or die.*

I hold the note up to show Lucas. "See? That woman left this here, just now. It's a warning telling us we have to go!"

He squints at the note, then looks at me like I'm insane. "Will you just get back in here?"

I clutch the note, making my way back around the house, my mind spinning. If the woman in the deer mask is real, then what else is real? Was that really a hair-doll Lucas found in the cave yesterday? My mouth fills with a sharp metallic taste. I shove the note in my pocket. We have to get the hell out of here.

When I get back into the cabin, Heather and Eli are standing in the kitchen, making coffee. Lucas sits at the counter, his arms crossed, his whole body tense.

"You alright, Sade?" Heather asks. "Lucas mentioned you ran outside looking for someone." She sets a coffee mug down for me.

"Yes, I did, and we need to leave, right now."

"What?" Heather's head cocks to the side. Her eyes flick to Lucas.

He lets out a heavy sigh and massages his brow.

"We're not safe here." My voice starts to tremble. "I saw a woman earlier this morning in the woods. Then she followed me back to the cabin. She was at our window, just now."

"Where did she go?" Eli asks, no sense of urgency to his tone. He starts filling his coffee cup, like he has no intention of leaving.

I groan. "I don't know! But she said we need to leave, and we have to listen to her, please." I grab Lucas's arm, trying to pull him up. "Just trust me—I know what I'm talking about."

Lucas yanks his arm from me. "I didn't even *see* this woman! Seriously, why are you being like this?" He gestures at me, his hands moving up and down in bewildered frustration like I'm wearing a clown costume.

Heather and Eli make eye contact. Heather frowns. "Why did she say we need to go exactly?"

"She didn't explain, but she left a note. I-I've seen one like it." I stop, trying to steady my breath. "It sounds crazy, but I know what I'm talking about. I'm sorry to cut the weekend short—"

"We are not leaving." Lucas glares at me, his anger meter teetering at 95 percent. Just a little more and he will start breaking things. But for once, I don't care. He can break things in the car.

"Can we see the note?" Heather asks.

I feel it in my pocket, worried that if I show it to them, they won't take it seriously, but I have to try to make them see that it's real. *But what if they still don't believe me?* What if they think it's a joke or something that doesn't have to do with us at all?

There's only one way to make them trust me: I'll have to tell them what I know, what I've experienced. I'll have to tell them who I really am, that I've been through this before. But first, I'll show them the note. Maybe it'll be enough itself.

I unfold the piece of paper, placing it on the counter.

There's a moment of silence while everyone looks at it.

Then Eli laughs.

Lucas does, too, but his is a strained, embarrassed laugh that goes on a moment too long.

Shame pits in my stomach. *They think I'm an idiot.* "I know it looks silly, but these are drawings of us." I point at the stick figures.

"This is clearly a child's drawing." Lucas scowls. "Some other camper must've drawn this and dropped it." He's speaking with such venom, some of his spit flies onto me. "This has *nothing* to do with us." He jabs the note with his pointer finger.

"Well, I can see how it looks like us," Heather says, her tone more curious than anything. She points to the skinny blonde stick figure. "That one is me."

"Yes, it is! And look: The threat is clear." I run my finger under the line *Leave or die.* "We have to go, Lucas, please." I clutch my hands together, trying to make eye contact with him, but he won't look at me.

Eli scratches his beard. "How about Heather and I go talk to this woman?"

"I wish I could tell you where she went, but she ran off." I grab Lucas's hand.

He pulls away from me and takes a step back, a vein pulsing in his temple.

"Can I talk to you alone?" I ask him. There's only one way to get through to him: I have to tell him the truth about me. I have to tell all of them, but I want to do this with Lucas privately first. Then, once he sees that I'm not just being silly and dramatic but am speaking from firsthand experience, he can help me convince Eli and Heather that we need to go.

"Please, Luke?"

Lucas grunts. "Sure, whatever."

I walk to our bedroom, Lucas furiously stomping behind me. Sweat beads on my forehead. If he's angry now, how much angrier is he going to be when I tell him I'm not really who he thinks I am?

I slip into our room and sit on the bed, gesturing for Lucas to sit beside me. He shuts the door and folds his arms, still standing. "What is this nonsense about needing to leave? You're really going to ruin the rest of the weekend with this bullshit?"

"We're not safe." I gesture at the note. "I know because—"

Lucas yanks the note from my hands. His eyebrows rise in

amused intrigue. "I can't believe this is what you're all worked up about." He flaps the note in my face, then rips it in half.

I gasp, jumping up to stop him, but the note is already in two pieces. I can see how to him the note looks like a kid's silly drawing, something benign that shouldn't be taken seriously at all, but he doesn't understand. "There are people in these woods who want to hurt us."

Lucas crumples the ripped note and throws it onto the floor. "How could you get worked up about something so stupid?"

I flinch. *I'm the one who gets worked up about stupid things?* But now isn't the time to get into that. I just need to get us out of here. I stand and pull our suitcases out of the closet.

"This isn't like you," Lucas says, a hint of concern edging into his tone. "You've never made a scene like this before. Seriously, Sadie. There's something you're not telling me."

He's right about that. The air becomes harder to breathe. The truth is like a spiny burr snagged in my throat.

I put my suitcase on the bed and sit beside it, gripping the back of my neck. "I know this is serious because I've seen a note just like it before. When I was a kid at summer camp." I let out a breath. That wasn't so bad. Now I just have to say the rest.

"*Okay . . . ?*" Lucas gestures impatiently for me to get to the point.

I swallow, trying to get some moisture into my mouth, trying to think of how I can articulate my next words to make it sound like I'm not a liar and a fraud. But there's no way to do that because I am a liar. I am a fraud. Delaying it any longer won't change those facts.

"My name isn't really Sadie!" I say in one rapid burst.

"What?" Lucas barks. It's unclear if he didn't hear me or if that is a reaction to what I said.

I inhale through my nose. "My name isn't really Sadie," I repeat, slower this time. *Keep going.* "It's Sabrina. Sabrina Evans. Remember the Camp Graywood murders that Eli and Heather mentioned the other night? I was there. *I* was the girl who survived. I had to change my name to have a normal life."

Lucas is silent. He studies me for a moment, his eyes narrowed, brows pulled tightly together. "This isn't funny."

"It's not a joke. Have you ever wondered why everything you know about my past is so vague? Why we never see my mother or any of my childhood friends or family?"

Lucas glances up, considering this. I can tell that, no, he hasn't ever wondered about that because 90 percent of our relationship and conversations are about him. That's why it's been so easy to hide my secret identity from him: He's always been the main character of our relationship. And I was okay with that. In fact, I preferred it that way, when we were safe. But now, I'm the only one who can save us. I stand, taking a step closer to him.

He holds up a hand to stop me. "Let's just pretend that what you're saying is true—so that means you've been lying to me for the past three years?" Redness creeps up his neck. "So, I don't really know you at all?"

He leers at me, the same judgmental, condescending looks he uses for waitresses who disappoint him.

My body shrinks. "I'm still *me*." I put my hand to my chest. "I just grew up with a really fucked up childhood that I didn't want you to know about. I don't even want to know about it—I've just been trying to forget it all."

Lucas throws his arms up. "I was going to propose!" He puts his hands to his head. "And now—" His voice cracks. "I don't even know who you are!"

At first, I feel a flutter of joy, then my heart and face fall like Lucas just slapped me. He "was" going to propose—past tense?

"Lucas, I'm still *me*. You still know me, you love *me*. You just don't know about the bullshit I went through seventeen years ago, but I'm telling you now. There are fucked up people in the woods and we need to go." My voice quavers. "I love you, Luke. Please, listen."

He shakes his head. "Just shut up, shut up!" He lets out an ugly whining sound that makes my chest hurt.

"I shouldn't have kept it all a secret, but I really thought it was for the best." I take another step toward him.

Lucas backs away, not looking at me. "I can't be near you right now. I need to think."

"Think about it in the car, please. Let's just get out of here. We'll talk about it more at home." Was telling him the truth a mistake? But what other option was there? I turn back to the suitcase, tears blurring my vision. What if we can't come back from this? What if our relationship is over? I wipe my nose on my sleeve. I can't think like that right now. First, we have to get away from here, then I can deal with us.

I unzip the suitcase, throwing our clothes inside. Behind me, the door slams shut. I turn around and open it. Lucas is storming down the hallway.

"Lucas!" I call after him.

He speeds up to a run, sprinting down the hall and through the living room. He yanks open the front door.

I go after him, stumbling over the rug in the hallway. By the time I make it to the living room, Lucas has already gone outside. I rush down the driveway after him.

"Lucas, come back!" My voice cracks, my breath quickening. *Where the hell is he going?*

He sprints down the trail, disappearing into the forest. I follow, my adrenaline powering my strides. But Lucas is faster. I keep shouting for him, but when I reach the part of the trail where the path splits, I can't tell which way he went.

Chapter 26

2006

Gríma Wormtongue pulled the knife from Allie's thigh. A spurt of blood sprayed out, misting the woman's pale skin. Allie buckled and thrashed, muffled screams escaping through the rag in her mouth. The woman rammed the knife into Allie's leg again, this time slightly higher. It made a wet thwacking sound, the same sound I heard when Mom ordered sliced meat at the butcher. Because that's what we were, weren't we? *Meat.*

Allie kept squirming, her spine arching, feet slipping in the blood. Her voice was stifled but I could make out the word she was screaming over and over: *"Please, please, please."* It didn't sound like Allie at all. It was too shrill, too raw, like hearing a dog in pain. I covered my ears, wanting it to be over, wanting her to die already so she'd stop making that awful sound.

Gríma Wormtongue continued to slice Allie in the legs and arms, missing the main arteries so she bled out slowly. Allie's head bobbed like she was losing consciousness, her eyelids growing heavy, but she kept squealing, *"Please, please, please."*

Finally, she went limp, face down in the pool of blood. Her limbs twitched like a fish I'd seen Dad kill by slapping it hard over a rock. "It's not in pain," he'd said, "the nerves are just firing one last time."

"Now, the teeth." Gríma Wormtongue licked the blood around her lips.

The man held Allie's mouth open while the women worked together to pull out Allie's molars with pliers. There was a loud crunching sound. "Damn it," yellow-toenails said.

"Don't clamp too hard or they'll break," Gríma Wormtongue hissed.

I clenched my hands together, my own teeth aching. Another *crunch*. My toes curled, my stomach rolling.

Crunch.

Then came a wet pop followed by yellow-toenails saying, "Ahhh. There we go."

They did Blakely's teeth next, pulling them out with ease since she never listened to my dental hygiene advice. Her yellowing teeth practically fell out of her loose gums, gifting themselves to the crazies like little gold niblets.

After they had enough teeth, the women cut the girls' hair, not all of it, but probably more than enough to make a couple hair-dolls. When they were done cutting Allie's hair, they left her body positioned on the floor so that she was staring at me with blank, glassy blue eyes. Her hair was cut all choppy, short tufts sticking out at odd angles, the kind of bad haircut I'd given Barbies when I was small. Allie's mouth gaped open, blood oozing from the holes in her gums. Her lips looked weird, loose like Silly Putty, all stretched out from the crazy woods people shoving their hands into her mouth.

That was the worst part to look at: her bleeding, drooping lips.

Then the women got on their hands and knees, swirling the blood on the floor in spirals, like they were making a gory abstract mural. I curled up, making myself as small and still as possible. Yellow-toenails inched closer to my bed, massaging the blood on the floor. My insides clenched.

She moved closer.

Closer.

She reached under the bed, scooping up the blood that had seeped under there, her fingers inches from me.

Yellow-toenails raised her head, and just as her eyes should have met mine, my whole body suddenly went cold, my muscles frozen in place as if I had been enveloped in snow. Yellow-toenails looked right at me, but no recognition registered on her face, like I was simply part of the floor. My heart pounded so forcefully, the rapid *ba-dum ba-dum ba-dum* deafening to my own ears, I thought she would hear it.

But she turned the other way, continuing her bloody finger painting on the other side of the room. The coldness lifted. *How? How could she not have seen me?*

The women started up their humming again while they continued painting the floor with blood. I sobbed silently, wishing this horrible ordeal would come to an end. They'd already killed the girls and took their hair and teeth—what more could they possibly need to do? Why couldn't they shut up and leave already?

While the women hummed, the man held thin bundles of Allie's and Blakely's hair over the candles. An acrid burning scent filled the air. I covered my nose with my shirt, but the stench in the room—the smoke, the burning hair, the blood, the body odor—was impossible to block out.

"The door is opening," Gríma Wormtongue said. "He is coming."

The man dropped to his knees beside the women, spreading his arms out, his head tilted up toward the ceiling.

"He accepts our offer," yellow-toenails said. Her head shot up, and her eyes rolled back in her head, showing only the whites. She grinned. "He is here."

I stifled another sob. What had I done? I'd let my friends be slaughtered by smelly, homeless crackheads. Lunatics who thought they were doing magic! I held my face and cried and cried.

Then I felt something cold move by my arm, a slithering sensation, like a snake was coiling beneath me. The blood spiral nearest me was moving, curling inward, rotating on the floor. I blinked rapidly, trying to see straight again, but all around the room, the blood was spiraling. The candles were moving, too, slowly spinning in place.

No way.

Were these crazy people really doing . . . *magic*? How else could this be explained?

The candles floated into the air until they were above the adults' heads, the pale wax raining down. The bed above me began to shake, the metal legs clanging against the floor. The dresser convulsed, drawers spilling open, clothes tumbling onto the bloody ground. The humming intensified, a low rhythmic tune encompassing the room, vibrating in my bones. The blood and candles spun faster and faster.

Then in unison, everything in the room went still. The flames of all the candles extinguished. They clattered to the floor.

Silence.

Darkness.

I clenched my hands, my nails digging into my palms. I breathed in quick little pants, trying not to make any sound. There was still a shred of light from the flickering night-light beside Blakely's bed. My eyes began to adjust to the darkness. In the center of the room, between the adults, a dark circle began to form on the floor.

A hole.

At first, it was the size of a fist, then it started to grow, expanding until it was manhole sized, and then it was a black crater, consuming half the space in the room.

The adults scooted out of the hole's way but stayed close enough to peer into it with wonder. Once the hole reached Allie and Blakely, their bodies slid off the edge, disappearing into the dark abyss.

The wooden walls of the cabin shuddered and groaned, like the wood had come to life and was stretching after a long nap. The ground beneath me softened, my head and back suddenly cushioned. I gripped the floor, and instead of hardwood, I touched soft soil. I scooped up a handful, the cool, fine dirt sifting through my fingers.

You liked watching her die, didn't you? a man's voice said in my head, the tone deep and rumbling. The voice sent all my hairs standing on end.

I shook my head.

You don't have to lie to me. I'm . . . The voice paused for a moment, switching from my left ear to my right. *Impressed.*

A cold, invisible hand stroked my hair, the same chill I'd felt over my body when yellow-toenails should have seen me.

"Are you the reason she didn't see me?" I whispered.

The voice didn't answer. But he must have saved me; there was no other explanation. "Thank you."

The metal bed frame above me wavered, like it was starting to melt. The blue sheet draped over the bed changed to a light brown flesh color, the edges red and bleeding, like torn skin. I looked closer. Tiny black hairs sprouted from the flesh. They started to wriggle, like the legs of a beetle stuck on its back. My whole body itched. "What's happening?" I whimpered.

Cold fingers gently gripped my head, turning me so I was looking toward the side of the room where the adults had been. The cabin walls had melted away, exposing a forest with upside-down trees, the roots curled in the air like gnarled fingers. A red moon illuminated the night sky.

The man with the sewn lips sat on the ground by the tree line while the women ran around on all fours with inhuman mobility and speed: their butts up in the air, hands clomping on the ground.

It would have looked kind of funny if it weren't for the shadowy figures running with them, spiny antlers sticking out of their heads, four legs as long and skinny as stilts.

Welcome to Hell, Sabrina.

Chapter 27

2023

I stand on the trail, shouting Lucas's name, searching for any sign of which way he went, but it's hopeless. The trees are too dense, Lucas's legs too fast, his ability to hold a grudge too extreme. The only way I'll find him is if he comes back to me, but he needs at least twelve hours to cool down.

The last time we got into a fight where he walked out on me, we were watching *The Lobster*. Half an hour in, Lucas said he was bored. I said it was because he just didn't get it. Lucas stiffened and said "Oh, so you think I'm stupid?"

I knew he wanted me to deny that, and I don't really think he's stupid, but I do find his taste in movies abhorrent. And I told him so: I told him that I don't consider Marvel movies to be "real" cinema and when watching a movie he should actually *pay attention* and not scroll on his phone. Lucas stormed off for two hours and gave me the silent treatment until noon the next day. And that fight was nothing compared to this.

If I'm going to find Lucas, I need help. I can't traverse the whole woods alone on foot, nor do I want to. My pulse spikes thinking of that note: *Leave or die.* What if Lucas ran straight into danger? What if crazy woods people are hunting for him right now? My breathing quickens—I shouldn't be out here alone and unarmed. I turn back to the cabin. Eli, Heather, and I can work together to track down Lucas, then Eli can talk to Lucas and make him calm down. Then we can all get the hell out of here.

When I make it back to the cabin, I stand on the welcome mat, my hand hovering above the doorknob. A small part of me doesn't want to tell Heather and Eli about this at all and would rather make up an excuse for Lucas's behavior: "He just wanted to go on a hike by himself!" Because once I tell Heather that Lucas ran out on me in the middle of an argument, she's really going to think he's an asshole. But her opinion doesn't matter right now, not when Lucas could be in danger.

I open the door and step inside. "Heather?" I peek around the foyer, speaking loudly so my voice carries through to the kitchen. "Lucas ran out into the woods. He—" I pause, carefully choosing my words. How do I make it sound like he didn't just storm off in a fit? "We had a disagreement over . . . look, I could really use your help."

I wait for a response, but it's quiet. The living room and kitchen are empty, but the coffee pot is still on. Where did Heather and Eli go? I check the hallway and patio, then press my ear to the bathroom door. Silence.

Maybe Heather and Eli left to investigate the woman in the woods right away, but I didn't expect them to go so soon or abandon their coffee. Eli's mug is on the counter, still full. Maybe Heather left a message.

I check the coffee table, the fridge door, the countertops, my hands growing clammy. *Where the hell are they?* I try to remember if they were here a few minutes ago when I ran outside to catch up to Lucas, but I can't recall. I was too panicked, too focused on stopping him.

It's okay, I tell myself. *Don't overreact*. But it's hard not to when I'm alone in a strange cabin in the middle of the woods. I inhale, exhale. Soon, I'll find a note with Heather's neat, loopy handwriting that says they'll be right back.

I check my bedroom door in case she stuck a note to it while Lucas and I were in there. There's nothing. I keep looking all over the house, but there's no sign of where anyone went, no reassurance that everything is okay.

The emptiness of the cabin tightens around me. What if I've been abandoned? *What if something bad happened to my friends and Lucas?*

Don't go from 0 to 100, I tell myself. They're adults. They can take care of themselves.

I walk back to the kitchen. The drawstring bag of cell phones is on the counter beside a fruit bowl. The current circumstance warrants breaking Eli's no-phone rule, though I'm not sure who I'm going to call if no one else has their phone. I open the bag and reach inside, hoping that if Heather and Eli did go investigate the woman in the woods, then one of them took their phone. My hand touches something jagged, sharp. *What the hell?* I spill the phones onto the counter.

My heart races, my throat tightening.

The phones are broken, the screens cracked.

This had to be an accident, right? Someone must've dropped the bag and didn't want to admit that the phones broke. *Or what if they were broken purposefully?*

Calm down. Don't overreact.

But part of me feels like I'm not overreacting at all—the phones aren't just cracked, but shattered. Smashed. The centers of the screens are caved in, like someone took a hammer to them. This was a deliberate act. Someone *wanted* these phones rendered useless.

I rub my temples, my stomach pitting. Who would do this? Eli? Or did the crazy woods woman break in here and destroy the phones?

I rush down the hallway to Heather and Eli's room. Tears well in my eyes. Everything about this feels wrong, too convenient to all be happening at once. I shake my head. *You're being paranoid.* There has to be a reasonable explanation.

I step into Heather and Eli's room. It's messier than I expected: piles of clothes and bits of trash strewn about, the bed unmade. Diet soda cans and empty kombucha jars litter the nightstand and floor. The room looks awfully lived in for just a weekend trip.

I'm not sure what I'm even doing in here, but I rummage through the bags on the dresser, hoping I find something that explains the broken phones, maybe some clue as to where they went. A backpack hangs on the chair. I open it, praying there's going to be a book in the inner pocket titled *Cellphones Are Bad for Your Friend's Brains: Secretly Break Them!* and soon Heather and Eli will be back and Eli will explain how he took it upon himself to rid us of our phones for our own good and soon we'll all be laughing about it.

I search the backpack, but there is no such book. I try the desk next, my numb hands knocking a cup of pens over. My chest is so tight, it hurts to breathe, and I feel like I'm a kid at camp again, Allie and Blakely in on some prank behind my back, laughing at me.

I pick up the pens I knocked over, but instead of touching cold plastic, my hands meet something soft, rubbery. Severed fingers litter the table, the flesh graying, dirt and blood caked under the nails. The room darkens and warps. I shut my eyes, pinching my forehead. *Not now.* I count to ten, inhaling, exhaling. *You're okay, you're in control, you're safe. The world is normal.*

But when I open my eyes, the desk has moved from the right to the left side of the room. The beige curtains have been replaced with a human torso. The back skin is stretched into wings, exposing a pair of pink lungs inflating and deflating. Something wet plops against my shoulder, and I turn to find it's the ceiling fan, the blades now severed human arms, flinging blood and chunks of fatty tissue and flesh.

I stomp toward the desk, bones snapping beneath my feet.

You always were ten steps behind, Allie's grating voice says. Her giggles echo across the room.

"Shut up!" I wave my hands in a stop gesture. I do *not* have time for this. I need to find Lucas. Need to figure out whatever the hell Heather and Eli are up to.

The desk has maintained its shape but for a half dozen eyeballs peering at me through cracks in the wood. The drawers are empty, except for the bottom one, which contains a leather-bound notebook, the cover engraved with a spiral. It looks like an item from the real world, not the Other Place. A diary, probably Heather's. I flip through a few pages but something else catches my eye. In the bottom of the drawer, beneath where the notebook had been, lies something silver and shiny.

Looks like Baby Bina's finally catching up, Allie says.

I shake my head.

There's no way.

It's not real.

It's just part of the Other Place, like Allie's voice, like all of this.

It is real. Damon's breath chills the back of my neck. *You are so close to the truth.*

My stomach drops, my vision blurring. The notebook falls from my hands.

Chapter 28

2006

A scream stirred me awake, piercing the fog of a deep, dreamless sleep.

My eyes opened, my vision unfocused. Slowly, the metal bed frame above me came into view. *I'm home*, I thought, *safe in my room under my bed*. Summer camp, the crazy woods people, Allie and Blakely dying—it was all just a terrible, vivid nightmare. I was going to crawl out from under here and find myself in my own room, my rats eagerly awaiting their breakfast. I scooted to the side and touched something cold and gooey. I turned to see what it was.

Blood.

Thick, drying blood.

No, no, no.

My hands shook. Memories from the previous night flowed back into my mind. It all seemed so hazy, too fantastical to be real. But the wooden floor was smeared with spirals of blood, just like I'd witnessed. The candles were gone, the adults and their belongings gone, Allie and Blakely's bodies—gone. The hole in the floor really had swallowed them up.

"Help!" Ruth stood in the doorway, facing outside, yelling, "Call the police!"

I crawled out from under the bed, drying blood sticking to my hands and knees. In the spot of the room where Allie and Blakely died, I expected there to be even more blood, thick wet puddles where they'd bled out, but there was actually less, and I supposed that's because it'd all drained into the hole.

I tried to stand, but my legs and body were too heavy and shaky, my knees wobbling beneath me. It took a few tries, and then I finally stumbled upright, bumping into Ruth.

She spun around, her cheeks pale, her eyes wide with panic. Relief flicked across her face, then her expression dropped when she saw my bloody hands and knees. "Are you okay? What happened here? Where are the other girls?"

I tried to answer but words wouldn't form. My mouth was dry, my tongue a wadded paper towel stuck to the roof of my mouth. I was thirsty, so thirsty it hurt.

"Where are Allie and Blakely?" Ruth asked, her voice rising. She squeezed my shoulders.

I swallowed, trying to get some moisture. "They're—" I managed to squeak out. Then I started to cry. My shoulders shook. Tears streamed down my cheeks. Snot clogged my nostrils.

Ruth hugged me, patting the back of my head. "You're okay," she cooed. "You're safe now."

I sobbed harder, pushing my face into her warm, soft chest. "They're dead," I whispered.

"What?" Ruth pulled back, holding me by the shoulders. Her gray-blue eyes searched mine.

I repeated myself, louder this time, though my voice was still hoarse, so the words came out a gravelly whisper: "They're dead."

Then, I laughed.

It started as a soft laugh that could have been mistaken as a cry. Then it evolved into full-on undeniable laughter. It wasn't intentional; it was one of those involuntary laughs. It happened to Mom once at Grandma's funeral—Uncle Jerry put his arm around her and pulled her away toward the hall and out of everyone's sight until her ill-timed laughter ran its course.

But I had no Uncle Jerry here to save me. Instead, my laughter escalated into hysterical cackling. Ruth watched me, one hand covering her mouth.

Tonya, the other counselor, rushed in. "The cops are on their way!" She stopped when she saw me standing in a puddle of gore, laughing with my friends' blood on my hands.

◎

In the counselor's office, two police officers sat across from me, one man and one woman. The male officer was older with a big bulbous nose, a scraggly brown beard, and yellowing teeth. He reminded me of Hector Barbossa from *Pirates of the Caribbean*.

"Start from the beginning of the night and tell us exactly

what happened," the man said. I could tell he was trying to be calm, soothing, but no matter how hard he tried, his voice was naturally harsh.

"Where are my parents?" I asked. I knew that wasn't the right answer, but I just wanted my dad and my own bed and my pet rats.

"They're on the way, sweetie," the woman said, her words twanging with a classic Alabaman accent. She was thinner with tan skin, poofy blonde hair, and big unnaturally white teeth. I felt myself scooting closer to her. Through the crack in the door, a sliver of Ruth's side was visible as she eavesdropped, but I didn't rat her out. I would've eavesdropped too.

"Look, the sooner you tell us what happened"—Officer Barbossa tapped his pen impatiently on the desk—"the more likely we'll be able to help Allie and Blakely."

Help them? How were they going to help two dead girls who'd been swallowed into the earth? I was about to say this, but the woman officer spoke first. "Let's start with a timeline, hun. Ruth said you girls had dinner at 6:30 p.m. and then went back to your cabin."

Ruth twitched at the sound of her name.

"What happened after that?" the woman officer prompted.

I looked down as I told them about how I went to the showers after I yelled at Allie and Blakely because they'd covered my mattress with syrup.

"So, when you came back from the showers, Allie and Blakely were already in bed?" the male officer asked.

"Just Blakely," I said.

The Mean Ones

The female officer wrote that down. "And where was Allie?"

"She was still outside."

"Doing what?"

"Kissing Jesse Pierce," I whispered.

"Speak up, please," the male officer said.

"*Kissing Jesse Pierce*," I enunciated.

"Who is Jesse Pierce?"

"A boy." My voice was monotone, my answers short and clipped.

The male officer glared at me with frustration. I looked down at my Converses, the whites stained with blood. These had been my favorite shoes and now I'd have to throw them out. I knew that was a selfish thought to have considering the circumstances. I should've been afraid or more upset: Normally, cops scared me. My only two friends in the whole world were dead. But I didn't feel much sitting there in that office; I worried I'd never feel anything ever again.

"The more detail you give us, the better," the woman officer said, her voice much softer than the man's. "This boy, Jesse Pierce, is a friend of yours?"

"Not really, no. I had a crush on him," I said, matter-of-factly.

"*Had* a crush? Did something happen?" The woman officer scribbled on her notepad.

"Allie kissed him. I saw her do it before I went back to the cabin last night. That's why she wasn't there." That wasn't really why I referenced the crush in past tense; the real reason was because the crush was before Allie and Blakely died, and already my life existed in two halves: before the murders and after the murders. Things from the before-times didn't matter anymore.

"So, you don't have a good relationship with Allie?"

I shrugged.

"Yes or no?" Officer Barbossa pressed.

"It's complicated."

"We'd really like a straight answer, sweetie," the woman officer coaxed.

I didn't want to admit that I wasn't on good terms with my dead friend, but what did it matter, really? "No," I said.

"And what about Blakely? She's your friend?"

"*Was* my friend!" I corrected, my cheeks heating from irritation and impatience. "Stop referring to her in present tense." I slammed my hands on the table, standing so forcefully I bumped my chair back. "She's dead!" Why were these cops so slow? I already told Ruth they had died, yet everyone seemed clueless. "They're both dead." I sat back down, crossing my arms.

The woman's lips pressed into a thin line. Officer Barbossa barraged me with a string of questions: What did you see *exactly*? Who killed them? What did the perpetrators look like? Did they have any tattoos or scars? Where are the girls' bodies? How did they die?

I answered truthfully with as much detail as I could remember. I told the officers about the bone knife and the smelly adults and their animal masks, how I'd seen the Gríma Wormtongue woman in the woods earlier and how the man had his lips sewn shut and how after Allie and Blakely were stabbed to death, a hole opened in the ground and swallowed their bodies.

At first, the officers wrote everything on their notepads, even slowing me down at certain points to get the details right. The male officer said "damn devil worshippers" a few times, but at some point between the candles floating up into the air and the hole opening in the floor, the police stopped writing and instead just sat back and listened, arms folded.

There was a moment while I told them all the terrible things I'd seen that I felt a release. I was putting all the gory images into words. I was being *heard*. Listened to. Believed. The tightness in my chest loosened and the tears returned to my eyes.

When I finished my story, it was followed by a long silence in which the adults stared at me solemnly. I thought they were simply taking a moment to process it all. I thought they believed me. I thought they would be able to help.

But that was when I was still a stupid, naïve girl.

Chapter 29

2023

Two and a half years ago, when Lucas and I had been dating for about six months, Lucas introduced me to Eli. They had met at the gym a few months prior and hit it off over a Viking's game playing on the TV. All it took was some football talk and a few late nights of *Call of Duty*, and the two were best friends.

The first time we hung out together, we went to a sports bar downtown, one that offered vegan options and traditional bar food. On the way there, Lucas let me know that Eli had a wife who was joining us. I worried that the wife and I would have nothing to say to each other, that it would just be me and this woman sitting uncomfortably while Lucas and Eli talked about sports and their online video game wars.

When we walked into the bar, Heather waved excitedly, her

rosy cheeks brightening. She was wearing an orange sundress and strappy wedges, her blonde hair down and wavy. She looked like such a typical, happy woman in her midtwenties. My mind went to the place it always did when I saw women around my age living their lives: Is this who Allie could have been? Is this the future Blakely could've had? Could *I* have ended up like this woman—normal, simple, happy—if I'd not been through the trauma of summer camp? I shoved the thoughts from my mind and remembered to smile and act like I *was* normal.

Heather and I shook hands, then we took our seats at the high-top table. Lucas and Eli started chatting about the basketball game on TV.

"So, Eli tells me you're a physical therapy assistant?" Heather asked.

I nodded and asked what she did for work.

"I'm a florist. I make arrangements for weddings, baby showers, things like that." Heather pulled out her phone and showed me her work. There were various flowers that I couldn't name, pinks and whites and yellows, presented elegantly in bouquets. The arrangements were beautiful, I supposed, the sort of thing I would come across on Pinterest.

"You're talented," I said. "Mostly I just massage old men and tell them to work out their flat pancake butts."

Heather snorted. "Honestly, most of my clients are basic bitches. I just slap together the same bouquets again and again."

I laughed, appreciating her honesty.

"Tell me more about your work. Are there lots of flat pancake men?"

"So many." I told her about my average clientele: fifty-year-old men with hip and back pain who were considering an unnecessary hip replacement. "About half of them cause their own pain by being lazy," I explained. "Rather than exercise and do the mobility work to make their own hips healthy, they'd rather just surgically get new ones."

"Wow. I bet hospitals prefer it that way so they can keep making money," Heather said. "If everyone was healthy, capitalism might just collapse."

"Exactly! Our medical system is so screwed up."

"Seriously. What got you interested in physical therapy anyway?"

The waitress came by to take our order, then I gave Heather the same lies I'd told Lucas about my fake happy childhood in Cedar Rapids, Iowa and how I always wanted to work in some sort of healthcare to "help people."

After that dinner, Heather and I began talking almost every day and hung out most weekends. She was so interested in my work, she and Eli were always down to do whatever Lucas and I wanted, and they even lived nearby, so it was easy for them to visit.

It never occurred to me how seamlessly Heather had slipped into my life, how easily she'd made me feel heard.

I'd never once questioned if Heather's integration into my life was perhaps *too* perfect. If Heather wanted anything from me other than my genuine friendship.

It never occurred to me until now.

Was this push for a weekend getaway in the forest not just

an innocent friend vacation, but something else? Something . . . sinister?

I reach into the desk drawer, picking up the shiny silver bracelet. It's dangly with several charms: a dolphin, a heart, a *B*, and another *B*.

The center charm is an engraved nameplate: *Allie*.

Chapter 30

2006

After I finished telling the police what I'd seen, they went to another room, leaving me alone in the counselor's office. A degree hung on the wall: Bachelor of Arts in Child Development, conferred on Ruth Dawson from The University of Alabama. Did they teach Ruth in those child development classes how to handle kids like me who'd witnessed unspeakable horrors?

I counted the lines in the grooves in the ceiling, trying to pass the time, trying to keep my mind distracted from the images I'd seen the night before. But the lines in the ceiling reminded me of how Allie and Blakely's blood had filled the cracks in the floor, and soon the cracks in the ceiling of Ruth's office were turning a dark red. Blood oozed between the wooden panels, thick warm droplets splattering onto my head and shoulders. The blood ran down my arms, filling the space between my fingers. I started to cry.

It's okay, that deep voice I'd heard beneath the bed said. *You're safe now.* A strong, invisible hand rested on my shoulder, the touch oddly comforting.

Ruth walked into the office; the blood and voice disappeared. Ruth frowned pitifully when she saw me crying and draped an American flag–themed fleece blanket around me. She left and came back with a Styrofoam cup of steaming hot chocolate, which I sipped for the next half hour. Then Mom and Dad burst into the room.

I'd never seen Mom look so relieved before, nor had I ever seen her out in public without makeup. She looked younger somehow, gentler, and paler without bronzer or her blemishes concealed. She and Dad both hugged me, squeezing tightly, and I realized how much I'd missed them, Mom's powdery scent and Dad's furry arms and shoulders, his big, hairy hands like the paws of a bear that could protect me.

I stayed in the office, gnawing the edges of the Styrofoam cup, making a ring of indents around it with my teeth, while the police spoke quietly with my parents in the hallway. I overheard words like *trauma* and *hallucinations* and *PTSD* and *child psychologist*.

Then we were in Dad's car and on the way home. I worried Nyarro and Radagast would be dead, dehydrated and starved. I thought that since I'd let my friends die, my rats would be dead, too, a sort of karmic justice from the universe. But when I got into my room, my rats were alive, clutching the bars of their cage. Their food and water bowls were full and fresh, and I appreciated

Dad even more for taking care of them. I cradled my rats to my chest, feeling some strange guilt that I didn't deserve them. They chittered and licked the tears from my cheeks. Then I slept for a day.

When I woke up and went downstairs, Mom was at the kitchen table on the phone with our health insurance provider, saying nonsense words like *premiums* and *copays* and *deductibles*. I wasn't sure what it was all about since I didn't need to go to the doctor. I wasn't the one who'd been stabbed.

"Sweetie," Mom said when she got off the phone, "we found a nice woman who's going to help you work through your feelings about what happened to . . ." Mom's voice cracked when she said their names. "Allie and Blakely."

And then I understood. I was going to a shrink.

Mom and I drove downtown to a big office building. I flipped through a *National Geographic* magazine while Mom filled out paperwork, then the receptionist led us to a floral-wallpapered room where we sat together on a squishy green couch.

An older plump woman with pointy glasses walked in and introduced herself as Dr. Brooks. Her gray hair was pulled up in a bun and she had a mole on her chin. She could've played Roz in a live-action version of *Monsters, Inc.*

"Sabrina," she said, sitting across from me and Mom. Even her voice was nasally. "Such a pretty name."

"Thanks," I said. My voice was small, tired. I just wanted to go home and be done talking to strangers, but it was nice that I had Mom next to me this time.

Dr. Brooks started with questions about my home life and

school, which I answered with brief, polite responses. Then she got into asking about what I'd seen the night Allie and Blakely died.

I answered with all the same stuff I'd told the police. Mom was stiff like a petrification spell had been cast on her, but when I got to the part about the man with his lips sewn shut, I noticed she was crying. I felt bad for making Mom cry, especially since I hadn't even gotten to the worst stuff yet. I continued, recalling how Allie and Blakely were tied up and stabbed, skipping the part about how I could've saved Allie but didn't.

Dr. Brooks listened closely, taking notes and nodding at all the important bits, like how the blood had swirled on the floor. She held eye contact with me and made empathetic "hmm" sounds. I found myself opening up more, slowing down and going into deeper detail. My stomach hurt and my nose got stuffy.

"Oh honey," Dr. Brooks said when my voice cracked at the part about Allie's teeth getting pulled out, the crunching sound they'd made. Mom winced.

The room started getting dark, the hairs on my arms standing on end. The ceiling light filled with blood, casting a red hue over everything. Dr. Brooks handed me a tissue box, and that's when I noticed it wasn't a tissue box anymore, but a small ribcage, stringy bits of jiggling flesh inside. She gestured for me to take it. I shook my head.

"What's wrong?" Dr. Brooks asked.

She seemed trustworthy, so I told her the truth about the ribcage in her hands. She quickly set it to the side. Mom turned to look at me, her lips pressed into a thin line, right eye twitching the way it did when I embarrassed her.

"What else do you see?" Dr. Brooks asked, leaning forward.

I told her how the bookshelf was now on the left, stacked with neat rows of severed hands instead of children's books. "The table is a man, twisted all wrong." My voice quavered. He was a couple feet from me, right where the coffee table had been. He was contorted, his skin spiraled, like someone had wrung him like a wet towel. We locked eyes, his bloodshot and bulging. "He's looking at me."

Mom barked a cry-laugh.

"I mean it." I folded my arms, turning away from Mom and the table-man, but everywhere I looked there was more gory stuff. I jolted when Allie appeared right beside me. She stood with one foot raised off the ground, her head cocked to the side. Her pink pajamas slowly darkened with blood. Deep, gaping holes formed in her skin. She opened her mouth and all her teeth tumbled to the floor. I shut my eyes.

"I think that's enough for today," Dr. Brooks said, softly. "Thank you for talking with me, Sabrina."

I forced my eyes back to her, trying to ignore Allie's bleeding body drifting behind her, the way her tilted head grinned sideways at me with her awful toothless mouth. The table-man started to moan and wiggle, his bones cracking.

Dr. Brooks gave me a soft, non-judgmental smile. I ignored all the chaos and smiled back. Even if Mom and the police didn't believe me, I was sure Dr. Brooks did.

I was diagnosed with PTSD and trauma-induced hallucinations, and written off as too mentally damaged and immature to help with the case. Dr. Brooks concluded that whatever I witnessed must've been so awful that I had to invent a dark fantasy world to protect myself from what really happened to Allie and Blakely. Mom gobbled up these reasons to explain away my "stories."

I felt betrayed that Dr. Brooks had listened to me so empathetically, only to turn around and tell my parents that I was crazy. But maybe I was. What if it had all been in my head? Wasn't that more believable than the crazy woods people actually doing magic? Wasn't it better if the gore-filled world I was seeing was something I made up?

Part of me wanted to stay locked up in my room and never speak of what happened again, but another part of me wanted to try one more time to make the police, Dr. Brooks, and Mom believe me. What more did I need to convince them? What if I could find someone who'd seen the same unexplainable things? Then that would prove to everyone, including myself, that I wasn't crazy.

I decided it was time to do my own research. I was only supposed to use Dad's computer for homework and *Neopets*, but he was still at work, so all I had to do was wait until Mom was deep into an episode of *Lost*, then I opened a private browser and googled "stabbing girls to death with a bone knife."

There was lots of unhelpful stuff about horror movies, some Yahoo answers, and suspicious-looking web pages I wasn't sure I wanted to open, but on the third page of search results, I found chat threads. I sorted through a lot of nonsense, but on page 12 of an unsolved mysteries forum, there was a conversation about a cult rumored to live in the backwoods of the south.

> Genghis_Kock: They worship some demon who feeds on children's souls and blesses his followers with youth
>
> BobbitWorm: That's an urban legend!
>
> Genghis_Kock: Its true. the cult flies under the radar because they only kill once a decade or so, plus no bodies. hard to prosecute a murder case with no bodies
>
> PearlHam: yah. the sacrifices are made to the demon Forneus
>
> Genghis_Kock: no that's the sea monster one. this is the forest one. Ralec. Ralac?

My eyes widened, my heart racing.

Ralac.

It was the first time I'd seen this word used outside the crazy woods people. I felt vindicated: It hadn't all been in my head. Someone else in the world knew about whatever it was that these crazy woods people worshipped.

Next, I googled "Ralac." The results were useless, links to a cleaning supply brand and a retirement community. So, I tried "Ralac demon." The first link was a Wikipedia page.

```
In the early grimoires Liber Deorum et Daemo-
num, Deos Inter Homines, and Spirituum et Terrae,
Ralac is listed as one of the three kings among
demons. In Deos Inter Homines, it is said that
```

```
Ralac's knowledge includes all things of the nat-
ural world, from botany to animal sciences to
"secrets" of the waters and earth. Deos Inter
Homines claims that his powers include the abil-
ity to bestow youth and beauty while the Liber
Deorum et Daemonum credits Ralac with granting
titles of nobility. Both sources state that he
will speak in his summoner's language but only to
one acolyte of his choosing. There are conflicting
reports over whether he is a natural born demon or
fallen angel. Spirituum et Terrae uniquely claims
that he has command over woodland animal life.
```

The page went into more boring passages that felt like a history textbook, but I had what I needed: proof that I wasn't the only person who'd ever heard of Ralac.

I picked up the phone and dialed the Hector Barbossa cop. He'd given me his number and email in case I remembered anything else that might be useful.

He answered on the third ring. "This is Officer Davis."

"Hi, this is Sabrina."

"Yes?" he said eagerly. "Do you have more information for us?"

I forwarded the chat thread and Wikipedia page to his email. "I just emailed you something important. I think it can help with the case. Remember how I said the weird woods people kept talking about Ralac? Well, I found stuff out about him on the internet."

"Let me pull it up." There was shuffling, static on the phone, the clacking of his fingers on a keyboard.

"The sacrifices are made to their demon," Officer Barbossa read aloud. "Forneus . . . No. Ralac. Submitted by . . . *Ghengis_Kock*."

There was a long pause.

I could feel him sneering through the phone.

My stomach clenched; he wasn't taking this seriously. "There's a Wikipedia page too."

"Look, little girl"—the officer sighed—"we'll add this . . . *fairy tale*"—I could see him gesturing in frustration—"to the evidence log, along with all the other magical stories you gave us, but in the meantime, we need real leads. Do you remember if any of the culprits had a distinct tattoo? A scar? Did they mention where this cult meets?"

I hung up.

After that, I stopped trying to research what had happened to Allie and Blakely, stopped trying to think about it at all, really. Mom and I continued to see Dr. Brooks, who kept trying to get me to talk about what had happened to Allie and Blakely without any of the "magical stuff" because "magic wasn't real."

Initially, I was resistant to how Dr. Brooks and all these adults were erasing the horrors I'd witnessed. But to please Dr. Brooks and my parents, I started to talk about how Allie and Blakely died without any of the magic bits, and when I talked about it that way, I saw less of the scary things. And soon, I started to remember it this way too. I even started to prefer the adults' version of events.

It gave me a way to explain the unexplainable things I had seen.

Chapter 31

2023

The Other Place has faded, the room returned to boring beige, the desk back in its original spot. Yet, Allie's bracelet is still in my hand. I throw it in the drawer and slam it shut, my heart hammering. *Why the hell would Heather have Allie's bracelet?*

I squeeze my head in my hands. *How* could she even have Allie's bracelet? It went with her body into the hole in the ground.

I suck in a breath, preparing to open the drawer again, hoping that it will just be a normal bracelet without Allie's name, that it was all just my demented imagination. I open the drawer.

Fuck!

It's the same bracelet, Allie's name as clear as the dolphin and heart and *B* and *B* charms.

Fuck fuck fuck.

I pick the leather-bound notebook up off the ground and flip through the pages, my hands shaking so badly, I drop the book twice. I hold the notebook open against the desk, my brain buzzing with so much chaotic panic, I can hardly read and make sense of Heather's handwriting. Finally, my mind manages to digest a line:

Sabrina Evans has assumed a new identity: Sadie Ellis. She still has the gift and seems unaware (or in denial) of this fact.

A metallic taste fills my mouth.

Sabrina Evans.

Heather knows my real name. How? Why hasn't she ever said anything?

I sink to my knees on the floor, clutching the notebook. My best friend. My only friend since summer camp. My only person other than Lucas, has been lying to me. Hurt and anger merge into a nauseating rock in my stomach. How long has she known my real name?

I flip to the beginning of the notebook. It's dated all the way back to several years before we met. I flick forward a few pages, stopping on an entry dated a month before that first meal together at the bar.

Our search is over, finally! We found Sabrina Evans. She's living in Denver, Colorado and working as a physical therapy assistant.

I blink and read the line a few more times, my heart plunging into an icy pit. Heather and Eli have known the truth about me ever since we met. Our entire friendship was staged. Heather was *searching* for me. For how long? And why? I wipe my eyes. I know why: Just like my mom, like Allie, like all those reporters, Heather wants to use me. My knuckles whiten as I squeeze the notebook.

All this time, I believed that Heather was a real friend who truly cared about me. But she's really just been another mean girl. She's probably somewhere laughing at me right now. Who is she planning to sell my story to? TMZ? Deadline?

I wipe my nose on my sleeve. I can't believe I let her into my life. I can't believe all the vulnerable things I've told her, like how Lucas is the first man I've been in love with, how my asshole ached for hours after Lucas and I tried anal for the first time, how Lucas likes it when I suck on his nipples. Is she going to tell that to TMZ? It's been nearly three years since she found me—why has she waited this long to sell my story?

I keep reading the notebook, pausing on the line *Sadie's boyfriend, Lucas, may be a prime vessel.*

Vessel? What? My head spins, confusion compounding with my heartbreak. I look over my shoulder to make sure Heather and Eli aren't walking in on me. I peek into the hallway to check that they're still gone. I'm alone in the house, but just to be extra careful, I lock their bedroom door, then I comb through the room, throwing open the drawers, which are full of clothes, much more than needed for just a weekend. I check under the bed, then feel through the pockets of the pants on the floor. I don't even know what I'm looking for exactly, but my friends are not who I think they are, and I need answers.

In the closet, I toss spare blankets and pillows out of the way until I find a mid-sized plastic storage container hidden in the corner. I lift the lid, revealing a messy stack of newspapers, polaroids, and printed pictures. I dump them out on the bed, spreading them across the mattress to get a better look.

There's a copy of the picture that Allie, Blakely, and I took the first morning at camp, the one with me in the middle after Allie braided my hair. The news articles are from the *Montgomery Times*, the local coverage of the Graywood Mystery, photos and commentary on the press conference. I keep shuffling through the photos. There are more pictures of me with Allie and Blakely, ones that never made it to the main news cycles. How the hell did Heather get these? I suppose they were floating around on Myspace around the time of the murders . . . or could Heather have some connection to Allie's or Blakely's families?

I riffle through more photos. There's a photo of Allie, her mom, her uncle, and her sister on Christmas. They're all wearing matching green flannel pajamas, standing beside the Christmas tree with their arms around each other. My eyes land on Allie and the young girl beside her.

I never paid much attention to Allie's little sister. But now, I can't help but notice her small pointy nose and naturally platinum-blonde hair. Her intense blue eyes, even bluer than Allie's.

Cerulean blue, like Heather's.

Heather and Allie's little sister don't exactly look like the same person, but they could be. Faces change with puberty and age. I've gotten away with pretending to be a whole different person, so why couldn't Heather?

My breathing starts to escalate out of my control, my chest tightening, my arm muscles cramping from the anxiety. I count from one to ten, but the panic doesn't ease.

What do I really know about Heather?

I've never met her family. And what about what I heard earlier this morning when Heather mentioned her sister? She's never mentioned a sister to me—why else would she keep that a secret?

You're overreacting. You're going from 0 to 100, I tell myself. But my panic feels right. The signs are right in front of me. This isn't about selling my story to TMZ.

This is revenge.

Chapter 32

2006

The police said we didn't have to go to the press conference, but Mom insisted we show up to support Allie's and Blakely's families. Dad wore a suit and shiny shoes, his hair combed back. Mom put on a slim-fitting long black dress, a gray shawl draped over her shoulders, her hair in a low bun. I wore a simple but pretty navy-blue dress. Mom made me pull back my hair and wear a golden cross necklace.

"Don't let the necklace fall under your dress," Mom said, fixing my collar, making sure the cross was centered. "We need everyone to see that we're a good Christian family."

The old me would've rolled my eyes and snorted, but I didn't care anymore. I just wanted this whole thing over with so I could go back to bed.

The Mean Ones

At city hall, Blakely's parents greeted us in the lobby. Allie's mom was there, too, but she kept her distance, only giving us a brief wave. She was wearing heavy makeup, but the bags under her eyes were still visible, her blonde hair limp. Allie's Uncle Duane stood beside her, wearing a suit that was a size too large on his skinny frame. Allie's little sister was noticeably absent, and I was jealous that she got to stay home.

Blakely's mom looked as miserable as Allie's, her eyes red-rimmed, her skin puffy. But it was Blakely's dad who looked the worst: He'd gone all gaunt and gray, a ghost walking around in an ill-fitting human-skin costume. When he got near me, I hid behind Dad's leg.

"It's good to see you." Mom hugged Blakely's mom.

"I don't want to go on camera and speak to the press," Blakely's mom said, "but the police think it will help make people pay attention."

Mom squeezed her, rubbing her back. "You'll be okay. Just look at me when you have to talk."

Blakely's mom nodded, wiping her eyes. "I'm glad you're here."

"Of course," Mom said, still holding her. "Of course."

Now, I was glad we showed up: Mom was right—the girls' families needed us. "We're here for you guys." Dad gave Blakely's dad a firm squeeze on the shoulder, which I found lackluster. Why couldn't dads hug it out like moms?

Blakely's mom turned to me. "Oh, Sabrina." She cupped my cheeks. She had the same round eyes as Blakely, the same auburn shade of hair. A jolt of pain hit my chest. I looked at my feet.

"I'm so glad you're—" Blakely's mom's voice broke off, a mix of emotions edging into her tone. Was she mad that I was alive and not Blakely? Jealous? I would be. She cleared her throat. "So glad you're okay."

The police chief walked into the hallway. His badge read Duke Sullivan, and he was at least half a foot taller than Dad, and very round but only in the middle, like a pregnant woman. He had a bushy brown mustache that looked like a wooly caterpillar had died above his upper lip. He gestured for all of us to follow him. "We're starting."

In the auditorium, Mom, Dad, and I sat in a row of chairs off to the side, out of the way of the local news stations set up throughout the room.

On the stage against a black backdrop were two giant framed photos of Allie and Blakely on picture day, both wearing pink shirts, their hair crimped. I glanced away from the pictures, their faces too big, too difficult for me to look at, the memory of us crimping our hair together that morning replaying in my mind. Allie had done the back parts of my hair that I couldn't reach. I swallowed the lump in my throat.

Duke Sullivan stood in the center of the stage at a wooden podium. Allie's mom and uncle stood to his left, Blakely's parents to his right. Cameras flashed. Microphones were set up throughout the room. There were so many people all around. My hands were sweaty, my stomach a sour pit.

Duke Sullivan spoke into a mic, introducing himself and the other officers on the case, his voice slow and deep. Then he said things about this tragedy likely being the work of a devil cult, and the importance of God, family, community, and God again. It went on a long, long time and felt even longer because of Duke's Southern drawl.

My stomach pain dulled, replaced with great boredom and fatigue. My shoulders slouched. My head started bobbing down. Mom bumped me with her elbow, her touch telling me to sit up straight, look sad, *look proper*!

I pulled my shoulders back, and blinked, forcing myself to stay awake. It wasn't that Allie and Blakely's death bored me, it was just that this event was one of those painfully dull adult things no child wants to be at, like going to the DMV, but much more serious. I remembered that Allie's and Blakely's parents were there, and I tilted my chin up, looking sad but alert.

"We will not rest until we've brought Allie and Blakely home," Duke said, which I thought was a hopeful sign that he was finally wrapping up his speech. "We are investigating all leads. If you have any information at all, please come forward. There's a tip line and a website."

"What about the witness?!" a reporter shouted. "What did she see?"

More reporters called out in agreement.

Mom sat up straighter, her posture saying *That's us. We're here*!

Dad gripped my shoulder, giving me a reassuring squeeze.

"We won't be releasing any of that information to the public," Duke said. "But she has been very helpful, and whoever took the girls *will* be caught."

I rolled my eyes. Because the bodies weren't found, the police were still acting like the girls were just "missing" and not dead.

Duke droned on a bit more about responsibility and punishment and money for a reward. Then he took a step back, letting Allie's and Blakely's parents move up to the podium.

"I just want my baby home," Allie's mom said into the microphone. She sobbed, feedback screeching across the room. "Please, if you know anything at all, help us bring our little girl back."

I squirmed in my seat.

"Allie—if you're out there, we love you," her uncle said.

Blakely's mom and dad said similar things, except her dad's voice was numb, nearly monotone except for when his voice cracked saying Blakely's name. Duke Sullivan inched his way back to the mic and said a few more closing notes. Then finally, the press conference ended.

Allie's and Blakely's families left the stage toward the back. Several reporters went after them. Dad and I headed for the exit while Mom walked slowly behind us, craning her head toward the news crews.

"Aren't we lucky to have our daughter home safe?" Mom said to Dad, practically shouting. "Can you imagine if Sabrina didn't make it back from Camp Graywood either?"

A reporter's head snapped Mom's way. "Your daughter was at Camp Graywood?"

"Oh god," Dad muttered under his breath.

"Yes," Mom said. "We're very fortunate that she wasn't hurt too." She put her hand on my shoulder.

The reporter, a fair-skinned woman in a black pencil skirt, turned to me. "You were friends with Allie and Blakely?"

"Yeah," I said.

"Best friends," Mom corrected. She wiped her cheeks.

"Were you in their cabin?" the reporter asked.

Before I could answer, other reporters were shouting questions, heading our way, forming a circle around us.

"Is that the survivor?"

"Oh my god—the witness is here!"

Cameras swung our direction and started clicking. A man held a mic in Mom's face. "How does it feel to have your daughter home, Mrs. Evans?"

Dad tried to steer us away, but Mom planted her feet, holding Dad's arm.

"We are just so blessed that Sabrina came home safe," Mom spoke into the mic. "God was watching our daughter that night." She dabbed her eyes.

I cringed. Mom was too oblivious to see how her words made it sound like God didn't care about Allie or Blakely.

"How did it feel when you realized it was your daughter who had lived?" another reporter asked.

Mom gave a blubbering answer with lots of dramatic pauses. I folded my arms, bored and annoyed that we still had to be here. Dad was quiet and gave a firm nod here and there. He shifted his body to shield me from the direct questions, but more reporters were crowding around us.

"And what about you, little girl?" a reporter asked, shoving a mic under Dad's arm and into my face. "If Allie and Blakely are out there watching this right now, what would you want to say to them?"

They aren't watching. This whole thing was a waste of time.

Dad tried to wave the reporter off, but Mom said, "Let her speak."

I was tired. Physically, mentally, emotionally. My feet hurt from the dress shoes Mom made me wear. I was tired of trying to tell the truth with no one believing me. Tired of this boring day. And so I said what I felt in that bitter, cranky moment: "I'd want them to know that I never really liked them anyway."

The reporter jerked back like I'd bitten him.

Mom gasped. Dad ran his hand over his face.

My stomach walloped. The words had felt good coming out of my mouth, but now I knew I'd screwed up. Mom was going to be pissed.

"Oh, she didn't mean that," Mom said, laughing it off, her voice high and strained. "You know how girls are."

The reporter gave a half smile.

While Mom tried to do damage control, Dad seized the opportunity to take me by the hand and get us to the parking lot, nudging through the crowd, bumping people aside.

"You shouldn't have said that," Dad said when we got into the car. He turned around in the driver's seat to make eye contact. "That's the kind of thing you keep to yourself."

"I know." I groaned. "It was only to one reporter, though. It'll be fine, right?"

"I hope so," Dad said.

The next day, my image was plastered all over the internet: scowling with my arms folded. Someone edited my necklace so the cross was upside down. The caption read "*She Never Liked Them Anyway*."

The day after that, someone leaked bits of my initial police interview, and someone else told a reporter about how I was found alone in the cabin the morning after the girls went missing, laughing, with my hands covered in blood. Dr. Brooks had assured me that my laughter had been a perfectly normal trauma response, but now it was being weaponized against me out of context, interpreted like I found the whole thing enjoyable. Overnight, our whole town turned against me.

Death threats and hate mail started to arrive, page-long rants about our family being devil worshippers. Mom began throwing away all mail that wasn't obviously a bill. Sometimes, I fished the letters out of the trash, just to see how bad they could be. One from Allie's mom was addressed directly to me: a long-winded anecdote about how Allie was such a sweet, good girl who had pitied me and was my friend out of the goodness of her heart and would have been a doctor or astronaut if it hadn't been for me. It was signed:

I'll see you in hell.

—Scarlett Murray

Clutching the letter in the kitchen, my chest aching with memories of Allie's and Blakely's deaths, the world flickered dark. The apples in the fruit bowl turned to pulsating human hearts, the red tissue slick and glistening beneath the overhead kitchen light. A cold but gentle hand cupped my shoulder. *One day, you're going to be stronger than all of them*, the mysterious male voice said. *One day, you'll show them all.*

I smiled, relishing the company of my invisible friend, and the fact that I had been the one who'd lived. I put the letter in my pocket.

On the side of our house, above the hedges and below the bathroom window, someone spray-painted SATANISTS in dark red, the vandalism a stark contrast against our home's pale blue. Mom cried when she saw it. Dad painted over it the same day it appeared. I knew better than to tell anyone that I kind of liked it and wanted it to stay. Maybe, if we embraced our new label, people would be too scared to bully us. But Mom would never consider going through with that.

Not everyone turned against us. A few people were nice, thankful that I had lived. My homeroom teacher sent us flowers and a casserole. Dr. Brooks reassured me that when people were scared, they did mean, ugly things to feel in control, and soon it would all blow over. I tried to explain this to Mom, but she was living her worst fear of everyone hating her, and any viciousness at all eclipsed the kindness we received.

Over the next few months, we tried to return to normal. Mom started to go out again after she got on Xanax and dyed her hair from blonde to dark brown and started wearing oversized sunglasses, like a celebrity hiding from paparazzi. Dad homeschooled me for the fall semester. For the most part, we did return to normal. We acclimated to the hate mail and cold shoulders in public, like it was a bad smell we simply lived with.

And then the big fight came.

◎

Mom, Dad, and I went to Happy Lanes Bowling Alley like we used to for family night in the before-times, except we used to go with Allie's and Blakely's families, too, a whole group outing, so it was small and quiet with just the three of us.

We put on our stiff bowling shoes, the empty chairs in our lane an uncomfortable elephant in the room.

"So, who's up first?" Dad asked, overly cheery.

In the before-times, we used to have the kids go first, then adults. I tried to match his cheeriness and said, "I'll go first!"

I picked out a bowling ball from the shelves while Dad unzipped his bowling ball case. He'd been a professional bowler in college and had a whole collection of his own balls, which was humiliating. Last time we came to the bowling alley with my friends, Dad explained the nuances of the different bowling ball weights and the distinctions between plastic and urethane ones to Allie and Blakely. The next day at school, Allie said "Your dad is such a nerd. It explains so much about you!" and I'd burned with embarrassment, resenting Dad for carrying around his own bowling balls. But now, with Allie dead, I realized that Dad's bowling ball collection was actually sweet and endearing, the way he cradled and tested the weight of each one before practicing his strokes, his brows furrowed together in concentration.

On my turn, I knocked down half my pins, which earned me a couple minutes of tips from Dad, who went on to score a perfect strike. Mom managed to gutter her ball twice in a row. Dad laughed; she playfully slapped his arm. Billy Joel and Kenny Loggins songs blasted from the jukebox. My face hurt from using the smile muscles I hadn't in so long.

Our next game started. I approached the lane, readying the bowling ball, scooping low, like Dad had instructed.

"Look out!" Dad yelled.

By the time I processed what he'd said, something cold and hard crashed into my ankles, and I was falling, my legs swinging out from under me. I was still holding on to the bowling ball—my fingers twisted inside the holes, my thumb and pointer nails breaking. Hot, stinging pain reverberated up my nail beds. I landed hard on my butt.

"Strike!" a little girl's voice yelled.

I turned to see Allie's younger sister, Olivia. She picked up another ball, readying to throw it at me. Dad rushed to my side, helping me stand and asking if I was alright.

Allie's mom stood beside Olivia, and her Uncle Duane was there too. I hadn't seen him since the press conference. His skin was overly tanned to the point it looked crispy, and his hands were stuffed into the pockets of his jeans, which hung loosely over his skinny hips. He wore a red baseball cap and was chewing tobacco, his jaw moving continuously like a cow eating hay.

"Don't touch my daughter," Dad said harshly, not to Olivia directly but in the general direction of Allie's family. Mom rushed over, standing at his side.

"Where is Allie?" her mom asked, tears filling her eyes. "Where is her b—" she swallowed, the word "body" dying on her tongue. "Where is she?!"

A moment of silence passed. The family at the lane beside ours stared.

"Tell us!" Olivia shouted, stomping her foot in frustration. She looked like a tiny Allie with wider set eyes, the same bright-blonde hair and pinched little mouth. She stood with her hands on her hips the same way Allie used to. Looking at her, all the rage I'd ever felt for Allie came flooding back in. Hot anger flared from my broken nails up my neck to my eyeballs.

Back at camp, if Allie hadn't been such a backstabbing bitch, if she hadn't syruped my bed and kissed Jesse and hurt me every chance she had, then I would've shown her the scary note—we could've decided to get help together, we could've prevented the whole terrible thing from ever happening. But no, Allie just had to be mean, didn't she?

"She's gone. Dead," I said, my hands clenching into fists, "and if she wasn't such a bitch, she'd still be alive."

Allie's Uncle Duane let out a low whistle.

Allie's mom snarled. "You little cunt."

Mom gasped. "Don't speak to my daughter like that!"

Allie's mom charged for my mom. Uncle Duane turned his baseball cap around and stormed forward, readying his fist, but Dad punched Duane first, right upside the chin. Blood and chewing tobacco sprayed from his mouth.

Then Allie's little sister was sprinting forward and she was upon me, clawing my face and pulling my hair. I stumbled backward, my scalp burning. I landed on my back. Olivia straddled me, her bony knees stabbing my ribs. I shrieked and rolled over onto her, pinning her arms above her head. She was only ten years old, tiny and easy enough to hold in place. She kicked and screeched, "You're the devil!" Her spit landed in my eye.

I spat back, making sure it landed on her nose and mouth. "That's right." I mustered as much venom as I could into my tone. "And I sent your sister to hell."

Olivia started to cry. Beside us, Allie's mom grabbed a fistful of my mom's hair. The two women tumbled to the floor, side-by-side, clawing each other. Mom got on top, her fists holding Allie's mom's head, and she rammed her skull into the floor. Allie's mom cried out and shoved her knees up into Mom's stomach. Mom made a gagging sound and rolled over, sucking in air, and I worried that Mom had lost the fight, but then she stood, her eyes narrowing, pulling her shoulders back, fists raising.

Other families in the bowling alley stopped what they were doing and watched. A couple employees behind the counter shouted for us to break it up. I thought all the attention would make Mom settle down, but she rushed forward, screaming in a war cry, and proceeded to beat the shit out of Allie's mom. My mom didn't seem like herself anymore, her eyes dark, her pupils turning to scary little pinpricks, her hands punching and scratching, her polite, suburban Christian housewife mask completely gone.

I wondered if in that moment, while Mom busted Allie's mom's lip and ripped out a chunk of her hair, she already knew we would have to leave town and change our names, and so she decided to let all her rage out.

The manager of Happy Lanes grabbed Mom by the arms and pulled her back while another employee grabbed Allie's mom. A man restrained Dad, and the concession stand employees peeled me and Olivia from each other. We were all banged up, but no one looked as bad as my mom and Allie's, who were both breathing heavy, blood dripping down their noses, bruises forming beneath their eyes. Allie's mom's lip was split open, the swollen flesh shiny and purple.

"Stay the fuck away from my daughter," Mom said, her usually perfect-white teeth stained with blood. Mom's eyebrow was gashed, the exposed tissue puffy and red. She'd have a small scar there forever. I felt a mix of fear and pride that she'd gone into such an animalistic mode to defend me.

The bowling alley employees led us to the door, threatening to bring the police in if we all didn't leave immediately and never come back.

"Don't worry," Mom said, "you'll never see us again!" She kicked off her bowling shoes and I followed suit.

Allie's little sister scowled at me. "One day," she said, her eyes dark beneath her blonde bangs, a thin line of blood dripping from her nose. "You're going to pay."

Chapter 33

2023

Heather is Allie's little sister, and she's making good on her promise. The realization makes me want to puke. I was so blind, so stupid to not realize this sooner. Now, she's going to avenge Allie by doing something awful to Lucas. That's why Heather and Eli aren't here: They're out in the woods, hunting him.

I run to the kitchen and grab the largest, pointiest chef's knife, my entire friendship with Heather flashing through my mind. Last winter, when she and Eli invited me and Lucas to go on a ski trip, but Lucas couldn't get out of work—were they planning to do this then? Or that time we went kayaking and Eli's Jeep got a flat tire—was that planned? Was Heather supposed to lure us off into the woods but got cold feet?

I wrap the knife in a towel and put it in my backpack. I fill two bottles of water, just in case I have to spend the night in the woods tracking down Heather to save Lucas.

I rush outside. *Which way should I go?* Lucas's Mustang and Eli's Jeep are still in the driveway. So, wherever they are, they're on foot. I head down the driveway, running to the trail that leads into the woods, shouting Lucas's name.

No matter what, I'm going to save him.

This time, I'm not going to sit by and let the bad things happen.

Would Lucas save you? a small voice in my mind asks.

Of course, I reply, but my confidence wavers. I keep running, my pace slowing. Do I really have to save him? I could get the keys and get in the car and leave Lucas to his fate. I could feign ignorance, return to my simple, safe routine, and when Lucas turns up dead or wounded, I'll pretend that I never knew anything suspicious about Heather. Something about that is undeniably appealing.

No.

Normal Sadie, Good Sadie would save Lucas. And after I save him, he'll have to forgive me for lying about my past. He'll have to marry me.

The sun is fully in the sky now, beating down on me. I shield my eyes, standing where the trails split. I don't know if I'm running in the right direction at all. I take the water out, pressing the cold bottle to my forehead, trying to think straight. Which way would Heather take him? It depends on what she wants to do, I suppose. Symbolically, it would make the most sense to kill him the same way Allie died. That would make it the most vengeful.

But I have no idea if Heather has a small dingy cabin out here. And if she does, how would I ever find it?

I groan, kicking a rock. What's the next best place to revenge murder someone?

The cave.

It's naturally creepy with plenty of private nooks and chambers. The perfect killing grounds, right?

Yes, Damon answers in my head, his voice making me jump. I'm glad, though, to hear him in my time of need.

I sprint down the trail with newfound, adrenaline-fueled running abilities. When I get to the cave entrance, I look around for the tourists and hikers, someone to ask if they saw a handsome buff man being dragged away by a tiny blonde woman and a skinny guy with a man bun.

But no one's here.

The staircase is empty, the only sound a steady dripping of moisture from the stalactites plopping to the cave floor. I walk down the stairs, peering around the corner. The air cools, sending a shiver across my sweaty skin. The lighting dims the deeper I go into the cave. Where is everyone? Yesterday, several hikers were here. I don't like this. My shaking hands clench into fists.

I follow the stream, stepping carefully over the wet patches so I don't slip and fall again. The ledge comes into sight, the splashing of the waterfall growing louder. Every few steps, I glance around in case Eli's about to jump out of the shadows. *What if I'm wrong?* What if this isn't the right way at all and Lucas is out in the woods dying somewhere? My eyes fill with frustrated tears. I wipe them and kneel at the ledge.

Down here, Damon says, his voice carrying up from the waterfall. *You're so close, Sabrina.* A cool touch caresses my back, and my heart rate slows. I let out a relieved sigh. I just want someone on my side, and real or not—I have Damon. I turn to my right and left, looking for other paths to get down there, but the darkness is all-encompassing. And even if I can get down this cliffside, which way will I go? How will I find my way around? I don't have a phone. I don't have a flashlight. I don't even have a lighter. I groan, wringing my hands. How can I even be sure that they're really down there?

Then I see it: a faint orange glow. A fire. Deep in the cave.

Hope springs in me—this must really be where they took Lucas. I open my mouth to shout his name but think better of it. If he's being held captive by Eli and Heather, it would be wiser to approach stealthily.

"How do I get to him?" I whisper-cry out loud to myself, to no one, to Damon.

Trust your instincts, Damon says. I feel an inexplicable morale-boosting pat on the back. The absurdity of it almost makes me laugh.

I reach over the ledge, feeling for a rope, a ladder, anything. My hand touches something rough and cold. A metal pipe. My fingers follow the pipe until it meets another one, and I realize it's a ladder, bolted into the cave wall. It's rusted and old, bits of sharp debris flaking off in my hand. A thin piece of metal pierces my skin. I wince. This ladder is not up to the OSHA standards I would prefer, but it's my only option. I put a foot on the ladder, holding on to the cave ledge. The ladder creaks and shifts. I don't trust this thing to hold my body weight, but if Lucas and Eli made it down, then it has to be sturdy enough.

I take another step down, trying to ignore the groaning metal, the slight sway as it shifts beneath my weight. How did they even force Lucas down here? Images of Eli holding a gun to Lucas's head come to mind. I can't believe I ever trusted these people. My chest hurts. *I can't believe I thought they were my friends.*

I continue down the ladder, gripping tightly, taking slow, cautious steps. I want to go faster but can't. I'm blinded by the darkness, afraid that one wrong move will snap the ladder and I'll fall, if not to my death, then to an agonizing broken leg. I hold my breath, moving one step at a time, my hands slick with sweat and the slimy, humid moisture of the cave. Another step. *It's not so bad*, I tell myself, *not so bad at all.*

The light from deeper in the cave grows brighter. I can see a little now—I have to be close to the bottom. Something moves on the cave wall, dark and impossible to make out. There's a hissing sound, followed by scuttering and clicking.

I freeze, my heart rate ticking upward. *What the hell is that?*

I take another slow, cautious step down. A few inches from my face, hundreds of glittery black eyes stare back at me. Thousands of spindly black legs cling to the rock wall. I hold back a shriek. *Spiders.*

But these things don't have eight eyes. No. They have two beady little black eyes. They're cave crickets: They look like spiders with long antennas and huge legs—legs meant for jumping. *Oh shit.* I quicken my pace down the ladder. A cricket leaps onto me, landing right on my neck, its spiny legs prickling my skin. Another jumps onto my face, dangerously close to my mouth. I scream, smacking the bug off, and accidentally let go of the ladder.

Fuck. I'm falling.

Falling.

My stomach lurches as gravity pulls me to the ground.

I grasp for anything to hold on to, but there's nothing. I shield my head with my hands.

My back slams against the cold, wet rock floor.

The air gusts out of me.

My vision blurs, white spots flashing in my eyes. I suck in a small breath. My ribs ache from the blow, mid-back igniting with sharp pain.

What if I broke a bone (or several) and can't help Lucas at all now?

My blood goes cold, my heart racing.

Don't panic. Assess first.

I wiggle my toes, then flex my knees. Both seem to have full range of motion from this position. I push myself up. Shoulders and wrists seem okay. My neck can turn side to side. I probe my ribs and wince. They seem bruised, not broken. I exhale. *I'm okay.*

Crickets scurry over my legs, and I remember why I fell in the first place. Prickly feet skitter across my neck, sending an itchy chill down my spine. I scramble to my feet, cursing and brushing crickets off me in a frantic heebie-jeebies dance. My back is damp and muddy from landing beside the underground river. I turn around, trying to get my bearings.

A voice yells over the sound of the roaring waterfall. I listen closely.

The voice is masculine but strained in high-pitched panic. I crouch and walk toward the sound.

"Somebody help!" the man cries, and I recognize it as Lucas now, but I've never heard him like this before: hurt, afraid.

"Sadie!" he calls.

I'm coming, baby.

I continue toward his voice, walking carefully, the earth slick from the waterfall. Lucas's voice echoes through a narrow path in the cave wall, and through the crack, I can make out the firelight. To fit through this slim section, I have to take my backpack off and carry it behind me, then I step to the side, inching my way through the crevice. My back and chest scrape the rock walls, my pulse pounding in my ears.

I can take Heather physically: tackle her to the ground, bash her head and knock her out if I have to. Eli might be trickier since he's a man and has five inches on me, but he's a scrawny snowboarder type. Pound for pound, I'm stronger.

The path widens and I turn forward, walking normally again. I reach into the backpack, unwrapping the kitchen knife and gripping it with my right hand. The knife shakes, my whole arm trembling. *You're in control*, I tell myself. *You have the advantage.*

To help stabilize my nerves, I visualize what's coming: I'm going to step around the corner and see Lucas tied up by Eli and Heather. Eli might be holding a gun to Lucas, but he's not going to use it. Firing a gun in a cave is too risky; the bullet could ricochet or hit a structural rock and make the whole place collapse on us. Then Heather's going to start delivering a vengeful speech about how I let Allie die. She's going to reveal that she's really been Allie's sister all along and has only been my friend to get back at me. Heather's going to think she has the element of surprise—she'll think I'll be floored by this revelation, stunned and speechless. But I've already pieced it together. I know what she's been up to all along. *I'm* the one with the element of surprise.

My shaking grip tightens around the knife. I don't want to hurt Heather—even if the circumstances of our friendship have been contrived, even if she's been lying to me this whole time, a part of me still wants our friendship to be real.

Can we get past this? Is there any way this ends without more heartbreak, without bloodshed?

I round the corner of the cave. My chest seizes. A staggering gasp escapes me. I blink a few times, my mind whirring with confusion. The knife falls from my hand.

Nothing is what I expected.

Lucas is tied up—I got that part right. His hands are bound by ropes that are attached to hooks on the cave wall. He's strung up like he's about to be crucified. His skin is dirty, his shirt torn. His head hangs down, defeated. My heart aches; I've never seen him look like this.

What I got wrong—there are a dozen people standing around in the cave, all wearing animal masks: wolf masks, hare masks, coyote masks. One man has a giant moose head pulled over his own. The masks all look like real, poorly taxidermied animals, the flesh and fur unclean, drying blood caked around the eyelids and mouths.

Two people aren't in animal masks, but wicker masks made of woven branches and twigs, a small hole for breathing and two slits for the eyes. Somehow, these are even creepier than the animal masks. The people in the wicker masks lift theirs up, revealing Heather and Eli, and I get it: They have the vegan masks.

But who are all these other people?

What the fuck is going on?

Kneeling on the floor beside Eli is the woman in the deer mask who'd scared the shit out of me earlier. Her hands are tied behind her back, her deer mask flipped up over her head, revealing a middle-aged pale face, lips chapped and peeling. She glares at me.

Lucas's head lifts, his face brightening. "Help me, Sadie!"

"I'm here, Luke!" I yell back, keeping an eye on the masked crowd. "Just hold on!"

Heather smiles. "You found us." She turns to the others, her eyes shining with tears. "See? I told you. She has the gift."

What the hell is she talking about? "Let Lucas go!" I shout, trying to sound tough. I grab the kitchen knife off the ground, raising it with both hands to conceal how bad I'm shaking.

Heather raises her hands defensively. "Calm down, Sade."

"Quit talking and cut these ropes!" Lucas yells.

Eli walks over to Lucas and shoves a rag in his mouth.

"Don't touch him!" I yell, but Eli ignores me. Lucas thrashes his head side to side, his screams muffled.

I turn back to Heather. "I'm sorry I let Allie die!" I look around, paranoid that someone's coming to get me from the side or behind. "But you have to let Lucas go." I pivot back to Heather.

"This isn't how you get revenge."

Heather blinks at me. "*What?*" She looks genuinely perplexed. Amusement flashes across Eli's face.

I lower the knife, my head aching with confused panic. "You're Allie's sister. You've just been pretending to be my friend so you can get your revenge."

The masked people laugh, their voices echoing across the cave walls.

"Sadie." Heather walks toward me, putting her hands on my shoulders. "I'm not Allie's sister. Why would you even think that?"

I back away from her. "You have her bracelet. I went through your room. You know my real name. I heard you—you told Eli you have to for your sister—"

"You misunderstood," Heather says, getting closer, looking directly into my eyes. "You *are* my best friend."

"You're really not Allie's sister?" I ask in a small, cracking voice.

Heather shakes her head.

I'm filled with relief. Heather isn't Olivia. Our friendship has still been a lie, but not in the way I'd feared.

"My sister is there." Heather points to a small-framed woman in a fox mask. "She is here for the blessing."

"What blessing?" My head pounds with confusion. "Why pretend like you haven't known my real name? What is all of this?"

"Sadie, or I should say, Sabrina." Heather inhales and puts great emphasis into her words, like she's been waiting to say this a long time. "You are our oracle."

I'm too shocked to answer, baffled by what that could even

mean. Finally, I let out a croaking, "What?"

"We"—Heather gestures at the masked people behind her—"are the Children of Ralac. And you have the power to speak with him." Heather clasps her hands together. "Only you have the honor to enter his realm freely."

My brain buzzes with static. I try to find the words to respond. Finally, I manage to say, "I thought you were a Jehovah's Witness."

More laughter ripples through the room. The person in the wolf mask finds this so hilarious, she doubles over, and I recognize her platinum-blonde locs.

"You," I start, "I saw you in the cave the other day. You're all . . . ?" *What?* What am I even trying to ask?

"Let me explain," Heather says. "Ever since we found you in Colorado, Pike Forest has become a gathering place for the Children of Ralac. And like you, I had to make up a backstory. I became your friend to make sure you really have the gift. But it wasn't just an act. We really *are* friends." She reaches for my hand.

I pull back. Heather's blue eyes stare into mine, open and honest. "I'm sorry I lied."

There's truth in her words. She might not be who I thought she was, but she's no Allie. She's not a mean girl. These last couple years, we might have been lying to each other, but we are still friends. *Real* friends. Our thrift-store shopping trips, our brunches, our bad movie nights—they still happened. They still mean something.

"I never wanted to hurt you." Heather reaches for my hand again, and this time, I let her take it. She squeezes my fingers. I smile, the pieces of my heart sewing back together.

"Can we put this down?" Heather gestures at the knife in my other hand.

I nod.

She takes the knife, placing it on a rock. "I had to lie to you." Heather's voice cracks. "Because I had to be sure. You don't understand, Sade—Sabrina. We can't hear Ralac like you can. We have to use psychedelics to dip into his realm for a few minutes. We have to make effigies and offers and beg him for his presence. But he comes to you, willingly." She smiles at me with wonder, eyes shining. "Allie's bracelet—he gave it to me, part of my reward for bringing you here."

I try to process this. Try to form a response. My mouth opens and closes a few times.

"I don't believe it," the chapped-lipped woman who's tied up says. She spits on the ground. "She can't be our oracle. I've given everything to him." Her voice drops to a whisper. "It was supposed to be me."

"Shut up, Willow," Eli says. "John"—a guy in a bear mask steps forward—"take her and grab the sewing kit."

John gives a grunt in response, pulling the woman up by one arm, who wails again, "*It was supposed to be me!*"

"Willow?" I ask Eli, remembering the conversation I'd overheard through his bedroom door. "You know this woman?"

"She's been trying to scare you off," Eli says. "Hanging around our cabin, trying to get you to leave before we could get a chance to show you who you really are." Eli runs a hand through his beard. "I have to admit, I was skeptical about you, too, but ever since Heather first met you, she's been sure you're really Sabrina Evans, and I trust Heather. When I brought up the Graywood Mystery the other night and saw how you clammed up, I knew she'd been right all along." He puts an arm around Heather's shoulder and kisses her forehead. "You did good, babe."

An urge to simultaneously cry and laugh builds in my chest. I thought I'd done everything right to hide my identity, and yet. "How did you find me?"

"Your mother gave us your real name," Heather says.

I blink, the knife in my back twisting. "My *mother*?"

"She's not doing well financially and was posting online about your case, fishing around for interested ghostwriters and producers. She was more than happy to sell your name to us."

Anger flares in my chest. Of course my mother sold me out. I thought if I moved away for college and cut off communication, I could protect myself from her, but I was wrong. So wrong.

"How do we really know she has the gift?" a woman in a raccoon mask yells.

"Yeah!" the moose agrees.

"She found this place!" the coyote responds, apparently in my defense.

"So what?" Willow shouts back. "That doesn't prove anything."

"If Ralac chooses her," the hare says, "then let him show us himself."

"He'll come," Heather says, a sharp confidence to her tone. "He only comes to our plane for her." She pulls something that looks like trash from her bag, and then I recognize it: bandages, caked with dried blood. *My* bandages from when I'd slipped and cut my hand in the cave.

Heather kept my bloody bandages, not because she didn't want to litter like I'd assumed, but for whatever the hell this meeting is. The realization makes me laugh out loud, tears stinging my eyes. *My best friend is one of the crazy woods people.*

"The scent of her blood will draw him here," Heather announces to the room. She places the bandages in a stone bowl and lights them on fire. There's a moment of silence while the gauze burns. The metallic scent of burning blood fills the air. We wait. The gauze disintegrates into ash.

Nothing happens.

The crowd stirs. The person in the moose mask inches forward like he wants to eat me. But Heather's confident expression never wavers.

A sound echoes from deep in the cave, the deep, primal call of an animal. There's a snorting sound followed by the slow clomping of hooves on the ground. The people in the masks scurry backward, making a path.

A dark shape moves out from one of the tunnels, manifesting out of the shadows. It's taller than me, its brown fur sheeny and slick with blood. The thing comes closer, the firelight illuminating its form. The deer stands upright like a person, and I know what I'm looking at: the demon deer from the day I was lost in the woods. Its head is knocked off to the side, just as I remember it being all those years ago, the knobby bones of its neck exposed, stringy bits of flesh hanging from the vertebrae. Its antlers are still human hands, the fingers long and so pale they look translucent.

Gasps ripple through the room, then in unison, everyone

starts to slowly stand on one foot, their heads tilted to the side. I almost feel like I should do it, too, since everyone else is, but I stand firmly on both feet, my arms wrapped around myself.

The deer inches forward. Slowly its head starts to straighten, the strands of flesh worming toward each other and reconnecting until the deer's head is upright. The masked people start to turn their heads, too, everyone straightening their necks.

My body trembles. I inch backward.

Do not be afraid, Damon says in my mind.

I shake my head in disbelief. "It's really you?"

The deer doesn't respond. It takes another step toward me. Damon's voice speaks in my head: *Yes.*

I blink a few times, happy tears swimming in my eyes. He's not a PTSD voice. Not my subconscious. Not my "honest" voice.

Damon is real.

And he's always been on my side.

After the relief, I'm hit with disappointment: I'd always envisioned that if he were real, his true form would be a dreamy seductive man, something that matched his enticing voice. Not this . . . The monstrous deer corpse takes another step toward me. I step back, but a rock wall hits my back. I'm out of room. There is no escape.

"See?" Heather announces. "She can hear him. He's talking to her right now."

I have no human form, Damon says to me. *Not yet.*

Not yet? What does that mean?

"Ask him to sit," Heather says.

"Huh?"

"Do it. He'll listen to you."

"Umm, sit?" My voice cracks with fear and exasperation.

The deer stops walking toward me. It kneels, head bowed toward me, the broken nails of its pale antler-fingers reaching my way.

The room is silent, all the masked people watching me. Then all at once, they drop to their knees.

The woman in the rabbit mask comes forward, long black hair draped around her shoulders. She's holding a bone knife with both hands, presenting it to me. I don't want it; I shake my head. She lifts her mask, and my brows knit in confusion. *How is this possible?* I recognize her: Gríma Wormtongue from the night Allie and Blakely died. Her long nose, the high cheekbones, the waxy pale skin—it's the same person, but she doesn't look a day older. In fact, she might even be younger.

"How?" I start to ask Heather, not sure how to phrase what I'm asking. "How is she—?"

Heather squeezes my hand. "Ralac blesses us with youth for being his loyal acolytes. We worship him. We feed him. And now, we will be divinely rewarded. We've brought him his beloved."

Heather gestures for Gríma Wormtongue to give me the bone knife. Gríma Wormtongue places it in my palm, gripping my fingers and clasping them around the knife. She gives me a grandmotherly pat on the hand. The bone knife feels cold and smooth and unexpectedly light.

"You have visions, don't you?" Heather asks. "The world changes?"

"Yes," I admit. "The Other Place. How did you know?"

"It's Ralac's realm." Heather's eyes brighten. "He lets you enter to be close to you."

Ralac's realm? Does this mean I'm not insane, but I actually have . . . a special power? Seeing a hell-world isn't top-tier as far as special powers go, but still, it's not insanity. It's not a brain tumor. It's not a coping mechanism.

The Other Place is real. Damon is real. My head feels dizzy with revelations, my whole world tilting on its axis.

"And Lucas will be his vessel," Heather continues.

I massage my forehead. "And what does that mean?"

"Ralac requires a human body to stay on our plane," Heather says. "But he can only inhabit a body sacrificed by the oracle. Don't you see, Sadie? He wants to join our world. To be with you."

I look down at where the deer sits, but it's gone now, evaporated, a bloody puddle on the ground the only evidence it was ever really there. A metallic taste sours my mouth. I'm finally getting answers to the questions I always wanted to know, but still, I didn't ask for any of this.

I just want to be normal.

"But I don't want this—" I gesture around the cave. "I don't want to be an oracle." My voice cracks with frustration. "I just want to be a normal person."

Heather frowns. She wipes a tear off my cheek. "What's so good about being normal?"

"I—" I try to answer but can't. "I'm just so tired. I thought I was finally getting away. For seventeen years, I've been running from this." My shoulders start to shake as I sob. "I thought all this shit was finally behind me."

Heather grips my shoulders. "Don't you understand? With us, you *can* stop running. Join us, and you won't have to pretend anymore. We want you just the way you are." Heather hugs me, and then suddenly all the people in the cave are coming forward, reaching their arms out. I try to step away, but there's nowhere to go. Everyone's hugging me, all our bodies pressed together. The furry masks tickle my face. It's getting hot, too many bodies pressed against me. The smell of sweat and human musk fills my nose, but I have to admit, there is something cathartic and comforting about being held like this. My rapid heart rate begins to slow.

"We want you exactly as you are," Heather whispers to me again, and all the people in masks start to say it too.

"We want you the way you are."

"*We want you the way you are.*"

"I told you," Heather whispers in my ear. "You're special."

"You're special," the crowd chants.

"*You're special.*"

"What if," Heather says, "you gave up this idea that you have to be normal, and instead, you embraced everything you've been trying to resist?" She and the group take a step back, giving me space to think.

I swallow. I've never considered that before because it's never been an option.

But what if it is one?

A massive weight would be lifted from me.

I wouldn't have to strive so hard for something that feels unreachable and is so exhausting to try and achieve. And what if Heather's right: that the Other Place isn't something I should try and deny, but instead, embrace? Ever since Allie and Blakely died, I've felt some guilty pleasure in enjoying the Other Place, and what if I don't have to feel that guilt anymore? What if I can just enjoy it? That wasn't even a possibility before because it would've conflicted with being Normal Sadie.

But these people don't want Normal Sadie.

And now that I'm actually honestly thinking about it: I don't know if I do either.

I look at the people in the cave, their eyes behind the masks; they're beaming with awe, watching my every move, my every breath.

"You belong with us, Sabrina." Heather bows her head, then all the others do, too, like they did for Ralac.

"Our Sabrina is finally home," Gríma Wormtongue says.

All the others repeat, "Our Sabrina is home."

A strange, excited thrill fills my chest. I've never been looked up to before, never been accepted for who I really am.

A smile spreads across my lips.

"What the fuck are you doing, Sadie?"

I spin around.

Lucas has spit the rag from his mouth. He thrashes against the ropes, his face red, eyes bulging. "These people are crazy! Help me, now!"

My mind clouds with doubt. A moment ago, the choice seemed so obvious. But I hadn't been thinking about Lucas. He's in pain. He needs me. I try to regather my thoughts, but he's still shouting and getting louder.

"*Sadie! What are you doing just standing there—*"

"*Please, shut up!*" I scream at him, putting my hands to my head. "I need space. I need to think." Heather and the masked people take a step back, their eyes still on me.

For the first time in my life, everyone is looking to me to decide what happens next. For the first time, I just told Lucas to shut up. And it felt good. Really damn good.

"Don't you dare tell me to shut up!" Lucas snarls, thrashing his arms, kicking against the wall. "I'm being *tortured* over here! Now cut the goddamn ropes!"

I'm hit with the impulse to obey. I always do what Lucas says. It's ingrained in me, the connective tissue of our relationship. I take a step toward him.

"Hurry up!" Lucas snaps. "Walk faster!"

I approach until I'm standing a few feet from him. Lucas's chest moves up and down as he breathes heavily, his white shirt sticking to his muscles with sweat. Memories of our relationship flash through my mind: the first time he dry needled me, our first dinner date, how two days ago, he answered the phone in the gym, deciding for us that *Yes, we'd love to go on this trip in the woods*. In all these memories, I struggle to see myself, while Lucas is so clear; I'm a blur and he's the focus. Our relationship has always been about him, hasn't it?

What if it's time for things to be about me?

Lucas continues to shout that I cut him down. I tune him out, waiting for Damon to tell me what to do, to give me the answer.

It is your choice, Sabrina.

But I don't know what to do.

Do what you want. Trust yourself.

"Why are you just standing there?" Lucas's voice cracks in frustrated anger. "Do I have to spell it out for you?" He eyes the knife in my hand. "Cut the goddamn ropes!"

No, I think. And then this time—for the first time—I say it out loud: "No."

Lucas is momentarily stunned, his eyes widening, brows furrowing. "*What?*" he shouts so aggressively, his spit wets my cheek. "Cut these ropes, you crazy fucking bitch!" He kicks at the wall, twisting and writhing.

That ripple of disgust I've always felt when he acts this way comes to the surface, but this time, I don't suppress it. Instead, I let myself feel the full weight of my repulsion toward him until the disgust makes me want to vomit.

I take a step closer. I say it louder this time, sneering back at him. "*No.*" I tighten my grip around the bone knife, raising it to his abdomen.

"What the fuck is wrong with you—" Lucas starts.

You never listen to me.

You make me afraid to say what I really think.

To do what I really want.

But not anymore.

You controlling,

Insecure

Spoiled

Asshole.

Lucas's words cut off when I thrust the knife into his stomach. At first, the knife resists, his abs too tough. I've pierced the skin but not gone very deep, the tissue too thick to get through without real force.

He screeches and thrashes. "What the fuck, Sadie!?" The anger has left Lucas's voice, been replaced with desperation. "*Please.* Don't do this—"

The pain in his voice makes me hesitate, but only for a second. I rear the knife back, and this time, I ram it in as hard as I can. The knife plunges deep into his stomach, his blood spilling over my hands, hot and thick.

Lucas shrieks in pain, a deep, wet animalistic cry. He tries to kick me, but already his body is losing its strength. I've pierced his hip flexors, sliced his abdominal muscles.

"Sadie, don't!" Lucas cries. "Stop it! Please—"

"No." I yank the knife back, all my repressed anger from years of tiptoeing around him breaking free.

"Please, Sadie, I'll do anything. Whatever I did, I'm sorry—"

I'm possessed with a feverish wrath, and I don't try to stop it. I ram the knife in harder and harder, aiming for everything vital. *Thwack, thwack, thwack*. My arms burn from the force. His sternum breaks with an audible *crack* beneath the knife. Lucas screams so loud it hurts my eardrums.

His thrashing slows, his wailing quieting. His blood soaks my face, mixing with my sweat and tears. But they're not sad tears. I lick my lips. The taste is rich and salty.

I keep stabbing until my shoulder cramps and the knife is plunging into a pile of hanging limp meat. I step back, my chest heaving from the exertion. My hand loosens, the bone knife clanging to the floor.

Then chilling dread hits me, the post-kill clarity.

What have I done?

Lucas was all I had. And now he's dead. Because of me.

Now what?

I wait for the sadness.

I wait for the remorse.

But all I feel is a smile creeping across my lips, the electric pulse of adrenaline thrumming through my limbs. Then, most unexpectedly: relief.

I'm free.

I'm finally free of him.

My shoulders shake with laughter. Great sobbing, cackling laughter.

A hand grips my shoulder. I turn to see Heather beaming at me, the masked crowd behind her cheering. I was wrong: Lucas wasn't all I had. I still have Heather. And all these weirdos, apparently.

"I'm so proud of you." She hugs me and I squeeze her back.

"Now what?"

"We welcome him."

She pulls back from me, staring at Lucas's body. His blood drips to the ground, forming a large, thick puddle. It seems like nothing's going to happen, but then the puddle of blood begins to move, spinning around a small hole in the floor, like it's slowly going down a drain. I hold my breath.

A black wisp floats from the circling blood like a thread of thick smoke. The black wisp drifts up into the gaping wounds on Lucas's chest, and as it enters, the flesh closes, regrowing and sealing shut, the skin smooth and fresh. Heather takes a knee on the floor, bowing her head. I remain on my feet, holding one arm awkwardly across my chest, not knowing what to do with my hands or if I should kneel or stay standing or run away. My breathing comes in quick, sharp little breaths.

Lucas's head lifts slowly, his hair sticking to his forehead with blood. He smiles at me, his teeth stained red, his eyes completely black. Then he flicks his wrists and the ropes snap. Lucas drops to the floor, landing silently and gracefully on one knee.

I walk toward him, too stunned for words.

Lucas looks up at me—*not* Lucas, not anymore, I correct myself—but it's too difficult to wrap my mind around. The black eyes lighten and soften to Lucas's hazel, but they're not quite right. They're darker, the flecks of green gone, replaced with a gilded brown. I always thought Lucas's green-speckled hazel eyes were perfect. But these dark eyes are even better, like gold and chocolate.

I wait for him to stand, wait for him to tower over me and tell me what's next. But he stays on one knee and takes my bloody hands. His fingers are surprisingly warm, the grip strong. He looks up at me, holding my gaze for a long moment, like I'm the only person in the room. My heart drums in my chest. His lips press against the back of my hand. A tingling warmth spreads from my fingertips down to my toes.

When he speaks, it's with that deep, seductive voice I've craved and kept secret all these years. "My queen."

Epilogue

In the warm-up area at the Colorado Powerlifting Throwdown, Lucas massages my shoulders while I wait for my turn to lift on the platform. The woman currently squatting on stage is half a foot taller than me, lean and muscular, her dark hair twisted in Viking braids, a hairstyle for the undeniably cool and confident. A dozen friends and family are in the crowd, cheering for her. Maybe I should've done more with my hair than put it up in a messy bun.

"You've got this," Lucas says, then so softly, right in my ear, he adds, "Sabrina."

I smile, turning to look at him. I haven't gotten used to his darker eyes yet, but I prefer them. I prefer everything about this new Lucas, especially how I feel that I don't need him to complete me. I simply want him.

"Hey Luke!" A familiar voice calls. Walking toward us from the vending machines is Trevor, a physical therapist from the clinic where Lucas used to work. I groan, my pulse climbing. What if he notices something different about Lucas?

Trevor holds up a hand for a high five, and for one terrifying second it seems Lucas won't react, which will surely expose that something happened to the old Lucas, replaced him, but he reciprocates the high five, slowly and not at all like the real Lucas would have, but it passes as human enough.

"Bro, you competing?" Trevor asks Lucas without looking at me.

"No," I answer. "I am."

Trevor looks at me in surprise. "Cool. Good luck." He turns back to Lucas. "Man, I can't believe you quit. You doing okay, buddy?" Trevor frowns, taking in Lucas's paler complexion, the dark patches beneath his eyes.

"Yes," Lucas says. "Better than ever."

Trevor's eyebrows twitch, his eyes studying Lucas's face. Does he notice that his voice is deeper? But even if he does, so what? My anxiety over the situation evolves into some complicated pride. Trevor, in his banal, grounded reality, could never begin to comprehend anything close to the truth. I pity his simpleness. Some tiny part of me almost wants the truth exposed, so he and the rest of the world can know how I have risen.

"Umm, okay." Trevor scratches his head uncomfortably. "Well, see you later."

"Sadie Ellis," the announcer calls. "Opening on Platform B with 230 pounds."

My shoulders tense, my stomach backflipping. "I feel like I'm going to shit myself." I laugh.

"You won't." Lucas gives my traps one last squeeze. "And even if you do, it's fine."

I walk toward the stage, looking back at Lucas. His whole frame is sunken, his complexion sallow. He needs to eat soon. That's why Heather isn't here now: She and Eli are busy scouting campgrounds. I hate what has to be done, hate that Lucas has to eat even more to stay in this realm, but it's necessary for us to be together. I don't want anything to do with the sacrifices, though I have made one request, which Lucas says his followers have embraced as law—they only kill the mean ones.

Lucas gives me an encouraging nod. I turn my focus back to the platform and approach the barbell. I wrap my hands around the rough metal knurling. I step under the bar, securing the weight on my upper back, the cold metal biting into my skin. *I can do this.* I focus on a blank spot on the wall in front of me, like I do in training, but there are so many eyes in the room, so many voices chatting, so much distraction. My legs shake beneath me.

Lucas and I lock eyes, an understanding crossing between us.

The white wall I'd been focusing on darkens with decay, black veins spreading from the floor to the ceiling. The hanging clock fills with blood, rivulets dripping down with each tick of the long hand. The *Colorado Powerlifting Throwdown* banner has flipped to the other side of the room, and it's turned into a sheet of human flesh, blood trickling down the pale skin, raining onto the audience.

Everyone in the crowd blurs, their faces distorted by shadows, their voices muffled. Lucas is the only person I can see clearly.

My pounding heart calms. I take a step out of the rack with the weight secured on my back, then another, positioning my feet. I suck in a deep breath, squeezing my abs, then I sink into my squat. The weight moves easier than I expected, my legs bending, then extending powerfully. Lucas cheers, his voice the only one I can hear.

I return the barbell to the rack. When I unclasp my weightlifting belt, it's no longer made of leather with a suede finish, but dried muscle tissue adorned with teeth, held together by rigid interlocking human fingers.

It's absurd. Disgusting. But I don't look away, I don't close my eyes or wish any of it to return to normal.

I'm right where I belong.

The End

Acknowledgments

Thank you to all who've supported *The Mean Ones*, from its initial concept to its final form: My agent, Amanda Orozco, for being this book's earliest supporter and follower of Damon. My editor, Amanda Manns, for her love of this story and commitment to feminist horror. My writing group, The Ubergroup, and my early readers: Katherine Jennings, Michael Marquez, AE Kade, LM Sagas, Cindy R. X. He, Kelsea Yu, Meredith Tate, Camille Carine, Kassiella Kingsley, Lizzy Weber, Melissa Kendall, Laura Creedle, N.E. Turner, A.B. Rutledge, Suja Sukumar, and Kelsey Havlik. The cover designer Luísa Dias, cover artist Jocelyn McCall, and team at Creature Publishing. Thank you to Versa for being the best day job I could ever want, and to all the members who've been so supportive of my first book and now this one.

All hail Ralac.

Tatiana Schlote-Bonne is the author of the YA horror novel, *Such Lovely Skin*. She has an MFA from The Nonfiction Writing Program at the University of Iowa. When she's not writing, she's either gaming, lifting heavy weights, or teaching people how to lift heavy weights.

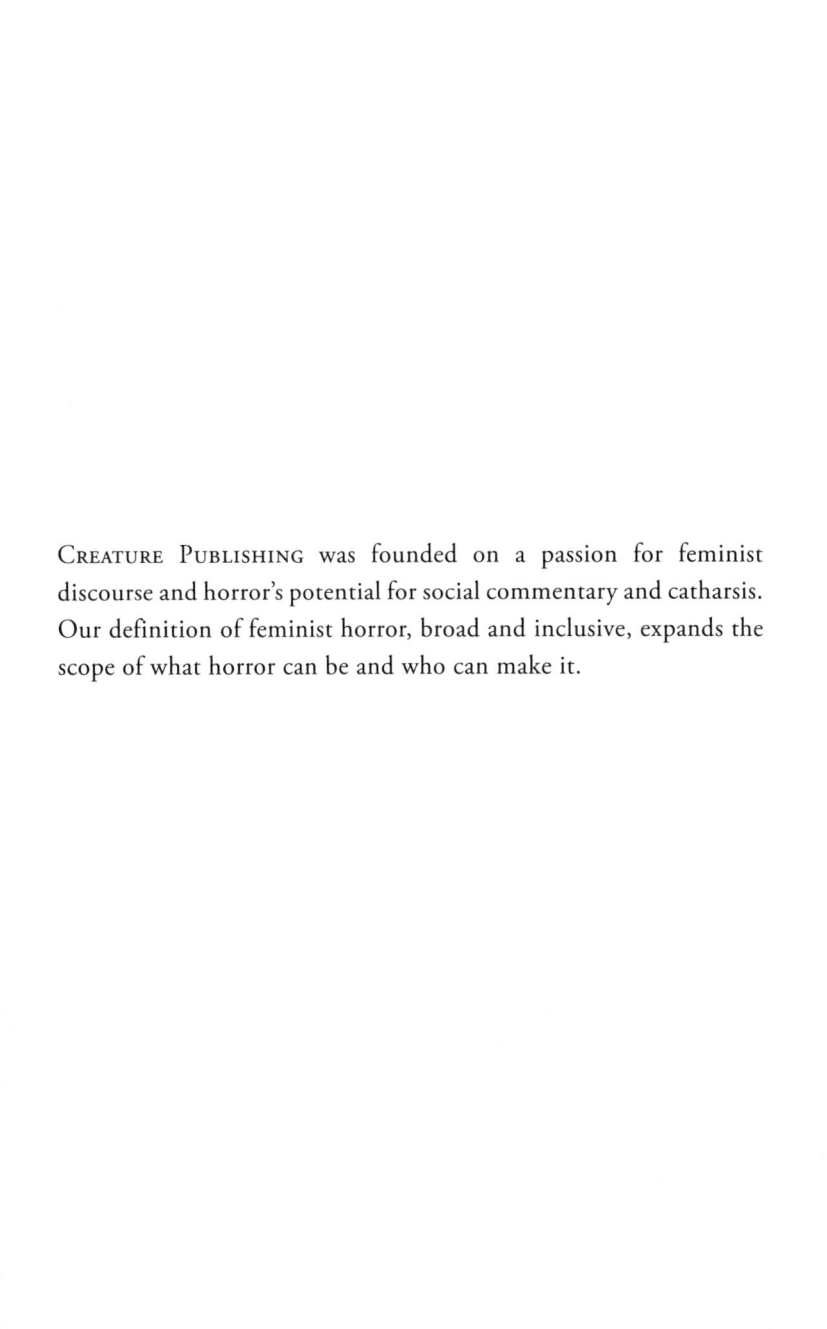

CREATURE PUBLISHING was founded on a passion for feminist discourse and horror's potential for social commentary and catharsis. Our definition of feminist horror, broad and inclusive, expands the scope of what horror can be and who can make it.